Councillor Hescot

By Brian W. T:

CHAPTER ONE

Melody Carnforth, collecting pots of plants from one of the greenhouses in the Middleton Hall Nursery, and loading them on to a flat-topped barrow outside, blushed deeply as Simon Spaulding, the supervisor, a pleasant-faced young man, smiled at her in passing. A quiet girl, with short dark hair and a slim boyish figure, Melody tended to blush quite a lot when having contact with any of her workmates, and Simon, having noticed Melody's difficulty, always made a point of being friendly to the girl.

The acute shyness from which she suffered was one of the reasons, though not the main one, why she found it so difficult to make friends with any of the men. Most of them found an attraction about Melody's appearance none of them ever experienced when looking at Carol Trennick, the other, older and less attractive, girl who worked in the nursery, but when she failed to respond to friendly overtures from even the younger ones amongst them, they gradually lost interest in making the attempt. Now, though she had worked in the nursery for about five months, she seldom passed more than an occasional word with anyone there, even Carol, who was the one planting the flowers in the pots Melody was collecting.

Carol was standing at the potting bench now, adding to another batch of plants already there waiting for Melody to collect, whilst Joseph Grubb sat on the edge of it, pulling thoughtfully at his nose, and professing the prophetic opinion to her that a change was in the wind.

His confidante nodded in agreement. Joseph Grubb was a morose man, with a pinched-in face and bony body that flinched from soap and water. A lack of personal freshness combined with a carelessness about where he found the food he ate, easily combining to corrupt his given name to the one by which he was known to most people. Maggot.

"It was bound to happen," The probing finger gave a nasal intonation to Maggot's voice.   "There was always going to be a vacuum when the Old Man went. Should have been me who filled it though. Should have been me instead of him!" He jerked a scornful thumb in the direction of Simon Spaulding as he passed the window of the potting shed.

Carol scooped up another handful of peat based compost. Despite having produced a glossy and expensively bound publication declaring a 'Green Policy,' which trumpeted its intention to join the movement away from depletion of the world's peat beds, the council had yet to change to the more expensive and less effective coir. Using the compost to fill a pot from the heap in front of her Carol pressed down firmly with her fingers again, watching her companion warily. Though much preferring the new broom, Simon Spaulding, to the stubby besom Maggot had become, she had to admit to herself that the latter had a point.

Middleton Hall was an anachronism. An eighteenth century landscape garden, with lake, woodlands, statuary and buildings originally designed by Humphry Repton, which had long ago been swallowed up by urban sprawl. The borough council had purchased it from its last noble owner during the nineteen thirties, when councils still had the funds to cover such extravagance. Now, in 1983, it was an uneasy mixture of olde worlde gardens and up to date recreational facilities, with the park, like most of the people attracted to work in it, forming a square peg in the round hole of a forward-looking Leisure Services Department.

Joseph Grubb, a prime example of the misfits and eccentrics the gardens drew in, had certainly served the regime of the old master well. Joining the parks department as temporary, part-time, toilet attendant one summer many years earlier, he had played on the meaner traits of his personality to rise swiftly through the ranks. The role of toady and informer was one that seemed to have been made for him. It should have proved a springboard to the staff appointment as Head Gardener he believed to be his by right.

Unfortunately for Maggot, it was not to be. With a rapidity of events which left the old misanthrope gasping like a landed fish, the borough was reorganised, Maggot's mentor opted for an early retirement and the new regime did away with the position of Head Gardener altogether. Bringing in a complete outsider as Supervisor instead

It had left Maggot with no alternative. By withdrawing his knowledge and experience from general use, he set out to bring down the usurper at a stroke

The result was quite the opposite. An outcome Maggot couldn't understand at all. It disturbed him enough to relent and offer advice to which his intended victim listened gravely, but paid no heed at all.

The attitude irritated Maggot by its casual dismissal of the quality and scope of his knowledge. A state of undeclared war, in which no quarter was sought or given, began to sour their exchanges. Meanwhile Carol, the only member of staff not making the most of the situation, fluttered alone and undecided in the no man's land between the two antagonists.

She was fluttering there now. Reflecting how typical it was of Maggot to be resentful of Simon for superseding him, without it apparently crossing his mind that Carol had an equal right to any resentment that was going.

Both in length of service and qualifications gained Carol was far ahead of Maggot. In his annoyance he completely overlooked the fact that she too might entertain ambitions of being in charge.

It wasn't just because she was a woman either. Carol could have forgiven Maggot if a display of chauvinism had been at the root of his attitude towards her, but it was not. The truth was that Carol had been amidst the flowerpots and potting compost in her overalls and donkey jacket so long her gender wasn't apparent to her workmates anymore. She was a person the world had forgotten was a woman. Maggot's attitude towards her, so typical of every man she met, was troubling to Carol's state of mind.

"Have you got a moment Joe?"

Startled from her reverie, Carol saw Simon standing in the doorway to one side of her.

"Of course Simon." Contrary to a fault, Maggot even resented the supervisor for being the only person ever to call him by his given name. Going to great pains never to show it, however.

"Peter wants a hand with those frames."

"I'm on my way."

"Simon…." Carol began.

"Simon!" Came a call from outside.

The owner of the name looked at Carol questioningly. "It isn't important." She retreated quickly.

Her companion hesitated. He had worked at the Hall long enough now to know that Carol could never push herself forward for whatever reason. It was this fault, had she but known it, which had led to her rejection when considered for the job of supervisor before Simon was appointed. Now she reddened slightly and turned back to the potting bench. With a shrug and a smile Simon moved in the direction of the voice repeating his name with increased insistence.

"It's that bloody Lovett again!" Len Saunders, the Senior Park Attendant, a tall, lean, man with an abrasive attitude, sat astride his bike, red faced and angry.

"Oh no! Where now?"

"Same place as before."

"He's not dug it up *again?*"

"Not so deep as the last time, but he's trying."

"Have you spoken to him?"

"You told me not to!" That was said resentfully.

"It's best that the two of us go," Simon said soothingly. "If only to substantiate what's said. There's bound to be trouble over this sooner or later."

"I'd like to put my stick across his shoulders and make it sooner."

"Which is why I don't want you to talk to him on your own. Leave your bike here and we'll walk across together."

Whilst Saunders was reluctantly acquiescing to this request, the object of his annoyance was waist deep in a hole of some six feet in diameter, digging furiously. He was a solidly built young man, more used to pursuing his twin relaxations of eating and playing video games than indulging in physical exertion on this scale. Sweat ran in rivulets from beneath the sandy hair, which lay across his forehead. A dark smear of mud, just above his eyebrows, marked the point where he had brushed at the constant stream with a grimy hand.

Arnold Lovett was not digging as an alternative to jogging, or simply to make life difficult for Len Saunders and Simon Spaulding. He was digging because he was convinced that beneath his feet lay buried treasure in the shape of the golden cockerel interred somewhere in the British Isles by the author of a book Arnold had recently studied.

In constructing his tale the author had joined a bandwagon begun a few years earlier with a golden hare. The plot of the story was not important. What mattered to the reader was that hidden amidst the text were clues to the whereabouts of treasure, which had been buried by the author, in order that it should be found by the first person to decipher the clues.

Arnold meant to be that person. Since reading the book pursuit of the cockerel had begun to dominate his life to the point of obsession. It had even cost him his job when he had been interrupted by his boss whilst programming the office computer to pinpoint the most likely sites for the

bird's burial. Unperturbed by his dismissal, Lovett put his
extra free time to good use. Devoting it exclusively to a
relentless search, which had seemed to pay off when
everything began to indicate a single hiding place only a
few miles from Arnold's home.

The fact that this chosen site was in the centre of one of
the main lawns at the back of the Hall was of little
consequence to the would-be discoverer of the golden
cockerel. It was gradually being brought home to him,
however, that it troubled the staff of the gardens a great
deal. He sighed as he looked up from his labours to
discover Simon and Len looking down at him once again.

"Haven't you got anything better to do?" The attendant
opened the proceedings angrily.

"Haven't you?" The other countered dispassionately.

"It's our job to prevent infringements of the bylaws Mr
Lovett," Simon broke in, before the retort welling up in his
companion's throat could find egress. "Digging holes in
the lawn is an infringement - as I've told you twice
already."

"So is rape," Arnold took the attack to the enemy.
"What are you doing about that?"

"I beg your pardon?" Simon regrouped behind feigned
ignorance of his opponent's standard riposte.

"Are you using as much energy in trying to catch the
rapist as you are in hounding me?"

"There is no rapist in this park, Mr Lovett." Simon
explained patiently.

"That's not what the papers say."

"Newspapers aren't always accurate in what they
print."

"The police seem to think there's something in it, even
if you don't. There are enough of them about the park these
days. What are they all doing here if the place is as safe as
you make it out to be?" With an air of having put Simon
firmly in his place, Arnold turned away.

Simon studied the prospector's back thoughtfully. "I'll tell you what Mr Lovett." He said at last. "I'll see if I can find one of them. Perhaps he can explain to you just what *he's* doing in the park, then you can return the gesture by explaining to him what *you're* doing here."

Arnold frowned at this sudden break with the traditional format of their exchanges. "Are you threatening me?" He demanded.

"If he isn't, it's about bloody time he did." Len, tired of seething in the background, made his feelings known by kicking at the heap of soil Arnold had piled neatly at the side of his hole. It tumbled, in a small avalanche, around the feet of the digger below.

With the best grace that he could muster, Lovett accepted the hint and threw his spade up on to the lawn. "You win this time." He conceded to Simon, as he followed it to the surface with slow dignity. "But I'll be back."

"Oi!" Len called after the retreating figure. "What about this bloody hole?"

"You have it mate - it's about your size."

"Forget it Len." Simon laid a restraining hand on his companion's arm. "Just fill it in."

"Better to fill *him* in," the other growled.

"I'll report it..."

"Yes, and he'll get a letter which he'll ignore, then he'll dig another hole and we'll be back to square one. It's a waste of time - and you know it."

Simon shrugged. "So long as they pay our wages does it matter how we spend our time?"

"It bloody does to me mate. I don't enjoy being put on by shit like Lovett. The Old Man wouldn't have put up with it, *I* know."

"He'd probably have helped dig the hole to prove there was no cockerel in it." Simon acknowledged his predecessor's eccentricity

"You know, you might have something there." Len's eyes lit up in sudden interest.

"Do you want to dig with Lovett?"

"No." The fire died as swiftly as it had flared.

"Then we'll just fill it in like we did the last time."

"You're the governor." The tone of voice belied the words.

Simon watched his companion for a few minutes to ensure he did at least begin the chore, then made his way back to the nursery yard.

Melody Carnforth, still loading pots of plants on to the flat-topped barrow as before, returned Simon's smile as he made his way past her to the sanctuary of his office and an illicit pot of tea.

CHAPTER TWO

It was some three days later that Maggot, hurrying to answer an insistently ringing telephone, left his toolbox unattended in the nursery yard. He was gone no more than a minute, but by the time he returned the tools were laying in a neat heap on the ground. Of the box there was no sign.

To say that Maggot was put out by the disappearance of his property would be to seriously understate the facts. The man was distraught. The box had been a family heirloom passed on to him by his grandfather, who had received it from an even earlier grandfather Grubb. An ornate affair fashioned from sandalwood; it was a work of art of which its owner was inordinately proud.

His workmates received the news with justifiable relief. Their assumption being that the unwary amongst them would no longer fall prey to the oft told tale of the making of the toolbox. Relief proved to be short lived, however. Maggot deprived of his toolbox was even harder to live with than the Maggot who had worshipped it with polish and cloth.

"Losing the tools would have been bad enough, but at least I could have bought more," he confided to Carol, as punctuation to every fruitless search he made. "It's the box that's irreplaceable. Did I ever tell you..."

"Yes." Carol cut in quickly, hoping, despite previous experience, that her curt response might dam the flow.

Maggot's eyes narrowed. "I don't think I did," he disputed coldly. "Not the whole story anyway.

It was my grandfather on my father's side who gave me the box, you see. *His* grandfather had made it whilst serving in the far-east fleet. Nothing else to do on long voyages in them days except work, carve or whittle something in your spare moments, sleep, then work some more. Quite a dab hand at making boxes he got to be. This one was special though.

My grandfather told me...."

His voice droned on along a well-worn path, but Carol was no longer listening. She wasn't interested in her colleague - or his missing toolbox. Carol's thoughts were of a far more personal nature, and centred on something that Carol herself had lost only days before.

Her life until that day had followed a lonely, but sadly common path. The youngest child of a family of five, to Carol, as the only daughter, had fallen the role of household drudge and mother substitute.

Not that the family had lacked a real mother in the beginning. It was just that Carol did the job so well, and with so few complaints, that her mother found herself gradually slipping into the background. Being left with a great deal of free time on her hands as a result of this, she began to pass it in the arms of the insurance man with whom she eventually absconded, leaving her daughter in sole command.

Carol accepted her lot fatalistically. Had she been either moderately pretty, or bubbling with vivacity and life, someone might have come along to rescue her from the drudgery, which seemed to be her destiny. But Carol was as plain in looks as she was in speech. So much so that no friend of her brothers had ever even considered her conquest during her formative years. As she grew older and plainer the chance of sexual encounters of any sort faded to the point where she no longer even considered the possibility of such a thing happening.

One by one Carol's brothers married and left home, returning only for brief visits during which their wives either patronised or pitied her depending on their wont. Her father lived on into his early seventies, accepting her attendance on him without compunction. He died without a word of thanks, the few worldly goods he had to leave being settled on his eldest son, rather than the daughter who had wasted her life caring for someone who proved to care so little in return. Carol was forty-two years old when life finally lifted all restraints.

It was a change to which she proved unable to adapt. Frightened by the enormity of the opportunity that faced her, Carol settled for a small house in which to live alone and a job in which she felt comfortable. Middleton Hall offered Carol a stable and unchanging environment, lacking any element of challenge or surprise. It had been what Carol thought she wanted until the Tuesday when Tom Stone had unexpectedly burst into her life and turned her insular world on its head.

Carol's dinner hours, like most of the remainder of her life, were spent alone. In the winter she would pass them sitting in front of the open fire in the women's restroom, either roasting chestnuts gathered in the varied woods of the Hall grounds, or toasting sandwiches as she enjoyed again a novel by Bronte or Austen. During the summer months, whenever the weather allowed, she would take her lunch out to a seat by the lake. There she would share it with the ducks, or an occasional rat from the colony based on the western island.

The warm May weather had flared into a still warmer June and the sky had assumed a deep shade of blue it carried, unbroken, for days. It was in consequence of this that Carol had established herself as the 12:50 to 1:50 occupant of her favourite park bench. Dedicated to a long-time resident of the area and former chairman of MEPS, sadly no longer living, it was situated close to the arched beauty of Repton's bridge, which still straddled the lake at its narrowest point.

A well-thumbed copy of '*Pride and Prejudice*' lay open on Carol's lap, but she wasn't reading it. Indeed she didn't *have* to read it, having done so so many times before that she could have repeated the text page by page verbatim. It was not familiarity with its plot, which was preventing her enjoyment of the novel, however. The image of the head and shoulders of a man reflected on the still waters beneath the radiant bridge was what distracted her.

Carol had been aware of the presence observing her during her dinner breaks for several days without being sure what, if anything, she should do about it.

One answer would have been to change her dinnertime venue. Another would have been to inform the park attendants of the persistent watcher and ask them to have a word with him. Carol had taken neither course. Whilst being aware of the probability that her silent watcher meant her no good by his interest, the novelty of being the object of someone's attentions - however unsuitable - was too strong for her to resist.

Careful to keep up appearances, Carol turned another page of her book unread as she continued to study the upside-down reflection of her admirer on the still surface of the lake in front of her. He really seemed quite attractive seen from that angle, she was thinking to herself, when her heart gave an extra strong thump and tried to leap clean out of her chest. The reflected head was moving across the water towards her instead of away from her as it had done on every previous occasion. She turned another page, and her hand shook so violently that she tore the paper and the book slipped from her fingers. Reaching down to retrieve it she became suddenly aware that a man had joined her on the seat, bringing with him a strong aroma of nervous perspiration.

"Hi," he said. And it was an apt description of his voice, which broke on an edge of nervousness even more pronounced than Carol's. "Nice day innit?"

Carol agreed warily that, yes it was. Unbending enough to follow the information that the newcomer's name was Tom, and that he was an artist who visited the grounds of the Hall every day in search of inspiration, with the reciprocal information of her own name and reason for being there.

"A gardener." Tom was small and dark, with shifty eyes, which seemed constantly drawn to the region of Carol's chest. His face had a damp shine about it, and when he wiped the palms of his hands on the legs of his trousers, as he did with great frequency, moist tracks followed in their wake. "Or a gardeneress?" He smiled at his own wit. "I always thought gardeners wore rubber boots. And rubber aprons sometimes."

"Sometimes," Carol agreed ingenuously, "but not in weather like this if we can help it."

"Pity." Tom stared out across the lake towards the rust coloured foliage of a tall swamp cypress. His fingers drummed an uneven tattoo on the arm of the bench.

"Why?"

"Oh," Tom's eyes darted from the distant horizon to Carol's breasts and then off into the distance again. "I was...ah..." the drumming of his fingers rose to a crescendo then suddenly died. "I was thinkin' of buyin' some boots - rubber boots - for meself like, an' I wanted to see what sort you wore in case I wanted some the same. You couldn't wear them termorrer, so I could 'ave a butcher's, could yer?"

"Well I suppose I could." Carol studied her companion doubtfully, "but..."

"Please." Tom twisted his hands together between his knees imploringly. "I know you must think I'm a pain but..."

So it had been agreed and though Carol felt very conspicuous the next day, setting out in the heavy boots with their red reinforced toecaps, the hour together had passed very pleasantly indeed. Tom hadn't been quite sure about the boots though, and so she had worn them again the following day. She had also worn them the day after that, the one after that and the one after that, until the memorable occasion when they had forsaken the attractions of the lakeside for a more discreet corner of the woods. There

15

Carol had somehow found herself lying on her back, wearing nothing but the boots, whilst Tom jerked and thrust into her body.

It was the beginning of a perplexing time for Carol. Sex with Tom became a regular feature of her days, and would have been enjoyable if it hadn't been for his insistence that she should wear her rubber boots on every occasion. His constant probing to find out what other articles of rubber clothing she had been issued with worried her. Especially when he wanted her to bring them with her on their clandestine assignations. Once she had made the slip of letting her beau find out about the rubber apron she sometimes wore when spraying insecticide there was no further peace for her unless she brought it with her when next they met. When she demurred, agreeing only to try to procure the rubber facemask that went with it, he became sulky and wouldn't agree to see her again.

Carol was uncertain what to do. She didn't want to offend Tom, and yet, even to a mind as inexperienced as hers, there seemed something very wrong about the request. She sought the advice of Melody on a private girl to girl basis and was offended when the latter tried at first to wave her confidences away, then burst into paroxysms of laughter when they were forced on her.

Carol was still struggling with the feeling that all was not well with her idyll. The letter she had composed with the intention of sending to Muriel Bainbridge, the agony aunt of *'Young and Modern'* magazine, still lay against the vase of sweet williams on her dresser at home, stamped but unposted. Riding the horns of her dilemma she had little time to spend on paying attention to Maggot's discourse about his missing box. Firmly in the forefront of her mind was the hope that Melody wouldn't pass on to anyone else the joke she seemed to have enjoyed at Carol's expense.

She need not have worried. The instant she had laughed Melody had caught the flash of fear in Carol's eyes and had regretted her insensitivity. Having lived too long with a fear of her own, Melody had no wish to inflict similar suffering on others. For a moment she trembled on the brink of holding out the hand of friendship and trust towards her companion, but the gesture foundered on the bitter reef of past experience and the moment passed. Carol retreated back behind a resentful silence and Melody left her to sulk in peace.

Indeed Carol was doing more than simply sulking as she watched the younger girl bending over frames to water the bedding plants which had been retained for the forthcoming sale. Carol was directing waves of active hatred towards Melody. Drawing in Simon when she saw him making his way towards the object of her attention.

"Men!" She thumbed soil into a pot with more venom than was necessary. "Hang around her like flies around a dustbin - and her chest as flat as a boy's! You'd think...." She tossed a handful of compost into another pot with a scornful sweep of her hand, then smiled spitefully as Simon's path towards Melody was ambushed by a heavy, bearded figure in a crumpled boiler suit.

Mr Gordon was the 'Old Man' of Maggot's narrative. The eccentric who had ruled Middleton Hall with such natural authority that old hands still touched their forelocks in reflex humility when encountering him.

There were a thousand and one tales to tell about Hereward Gordon. He was the man who had once invented a spade he claimed could dig in two directions at once. He was the man who had waged a costly but effective war against vandals by replacing every tree or shrub they damaged with a dozen others, until he broke their spirit and overwhelmed them. He was the man who extravagantly claimed varying careers as an army colonel, a marine commando and a naval commander during the Second World War, as well as a previous existence as Capability Brown. He was the man who intercepted Simon, as he was on his way to speak to Melody, and passed on some news. The vicious old rooster who had long ruled the poultry in Gordon's garden had disappeared during the night. Without any sign of a fox having been there to take him.

Simon listened as patiently as possible. Though Carol did him an injustice in thinking he spent more time than was necessary in speaking to Melody, he *was* in a hurry to see her. The account of the disappearance was long, however, encompassing as it did the qualities and value of the missing bird, and by the time Simon had escaped, Melody was no longer to be seen. With a sigh of resignation, he made his way back towards his office. The watching Carol, giving a triumphant twist to the last plant to be re-potted, inadvertently snapped its stem.

CHAPTER THREE

"Any chance of that mask you said you'd put out for the spraying I've got to do?" Peter Gilray enquired irritably.

Simon Spaulding, deep in conversation with John Death, the Maintenance Manager (South), looked round in surprise at the man who asked the question. "I put it out for you as soon as you asked for it. Hung it on the door of the tool shed next to the sprayer."

"Well it isn't there now," the other declared flatly.

Simon shrugged and looked at his watch. "You won't be wanting it until after dinner, will you?" He dropped a deliberate hint to Death, who frequently kept him late. "I'll get another one out for you then. I'd like to know where the first one went though. Are you sure it isn't there?"

"Certain. But I'll have another look if it'll make you any happier." Peter strolled off in the direction of the tool shed.

"Sometimes I just can't fathom the things that go missing around here," Simon raised a disbelieving eyebrow in the direction of his manager. "What on earth could anyone want with a face mask anyway? They'd only have to ask and I'd give them one without the need for stealing the thing."

Death made no response. Unimpressed by the depth of the problem as perceived by Simon, he was girding himself to confront a more pressing one of his own. "Is that *his* dog?" He demanded.

Simon smiled after the ragged black and brown mongrel trotting at the heels of the departing gardener. "Sammy? No. He belongs to an old lady living near the park who's pretty well housebound through arthritis. She turns Sam out in the mornings and he spends the days hanging about around here. He used to stay close to Charlie

Davies, but since he was transferred Peter seems to have been adopted instead."

"I won't have dogs at work you know." Death was feeling dyspeptic. The salad he'd had the previous evening had contained both cheese and onion, neither of which he found very digestible. His wife should have known that. Gillian could be absent-minded he knew, but he sometimes suspected that things like this were done deliberately, to make life uncomfortable for him. She'd changed since the last of their children had left home. He sometimes thought... No - that was silly! He was developing a persecution complex about her. About everyone really. Why *did* so many people he came into contact with seem to disagree with everything he said?

"You can't stop the public letting their dogs run in the park if they want them to," Simon pointed out reasonably enough, but disagreement was like red rag to a bull where John Death was concerned.

"Perhaps not. But you can stop the staff encouraging the creatures. It's just one more example of the lack of discipline you engender around you. You're weak Simon. You allow too many things to pass. I can see I'll have to take action myself if I want anything done about it. I'll draft a memo on the subject. And another thing...." Neither noticed the furtive figure slip past them clutching a carrier bag to her chest.

2

The relationship between Carol and her Tom had become more and more strained since she refused point blank to countenance wearing a rubber apron at any of their meetings.

At first her wellington boots and a pair of lightweight Marigold rubber gloves (ladies size), which she had found under the bench in the potting shed, had been enough to satisfy the demands of her lover. Dinner breaks then had become stolen moments of pleasure and excitement, the like of which she had never expected to enjoy at her time of life.

She could almost feel Tom's weight bearing down on her now and breathe the hot aroma of his sweat as she relived the feeling of pine needles pricking her bottom as they crackled and moved beneath her in the hidden clearing behind the Temple of Modern Virtue they'd made their own.

Lately, however, her beau had become distant in his appreciation of her responses and the waves of passion, with which he had previously overwhelmed her, had subsided into little more than a tidal eddy.

Carol was afraid. She was fully aware that she was very close to losing Tom at that moment and that the decision she had to make could prove to be a watershed in her life. When Muriel Bainbridge replied to her letter to 'Young and Modern' that nothing which took place between consenting adults in private was wrong, she knew that she must go forward with her man, or return alone to the barren life which had been hers' before.

With this in mind, it had been Carol who had appropriated the rubber mask Simon had left out for Peter to use, and who had smuggled it out on her dinnertime assignation. Her fervent hope was that it would have proved its worth to her before she was called on to pay a penalty for her crime.

There was little chance of her having to pay for what was likely to go undiscovered. The only person to notice her misdeed had been Melody, and she had no interest in Carol's behaviour, or the motives behind it. The young gardener was suffering a bout of acute homesickness sparked off by she knew not what.

3

Melody was a country person born and bred. Endless rows of buildings, however grand, and pavements seething with human life had always been anathema to her. Yet here she was alone amongst them, finding life to be a cold and friendless thing.

More and more since she'd arrived in the city; Melody experienced a yearning for the familiar. A face, just one face - it didn't matter whose – that she knew amongst the ranks of unsmiling people who turned the loneliness of her existence into a pain – physical as well as emotional – which ground away at her unrelentingly.

No point in her reminding herself of the reasons why she had felt it necessary to come here, and why it was impossible for her ever to go back home. Her arguments served to tranquillise the pain for a period, but only at the cost of it returning more strongly once the effect of them had worn off.

Join a night school class, or a club of some kind. Pretty standard advice to anyone citing loneliness as their problem. Melody shrunk from the former as being pointless in her particular circumstances and had tried the latter without success. Being left lonelier, if anything, by the experience.

For a while she thought that by chance she'd found what she sought in an all-night Laundromat, but Billy Danton had proved to be less than he claimed to be. Not Billy's fault perhaps, but it hadn't helped Melody to be let down yet again. It made her wary of any further attempt to slow the downward spiral in which she'd plummeted until she came to rest in the apparent haven of Middleton Hall. Now the need for something more was growing in her again and she was aware that a crisis was imminent.

Melody ran her mind over the alternatives still open to her, and found that the only one remaining was her religion. That frightened her. Coming from a strong catholic background, she believed God had possessed some dark reason of His own for singling her out in this way. In consequence, she feared the spiritual niceties of questioning that reason in His own house; but even more than that, she feared the purely human side of doing such a thing.

How would it be possible to go into the confessional and make someone else a party to a secret she never dared allow her mind to dwell on - let alone have her lips repeat it for another to hear? With no refuge to which to turn, Melody continued to fight her battle alone.

She was fighting it now as she passed her dinner hour walking the grounds, her mind anaesthetised by thoughts that took no account of the world around her, until knowledge of it was thrust upon her by a running figure who cannoned into her from a little used path off the Pharaoh's Walk.

Melody was no coward. If she had been, she would have paid more heed to the police warnings for women not to walk alone in the grounds until the hooded rapist had been apprehended. She had certainly never taken it to be a warning aimed at her. Not until she found herself falling, clutched for balance at the cause of her loss of it, and looked up at two eye slits in a hood on which was described a grotesque and terrifying face.

4

'The Middleton Hall Rapist', as the local press had dubbed him, had achieved his substantial notoriety as a result of what had almost been an act of whimsy on their part. Suffering a depression in newsworthy stories one week, the *Middleton Courier* had decided to attribute every recent rape within a five mile radius to a character who had been no more than a rather sad and inconsequential flasher in the park until then.

The publicity had worked wonders for everyone. The *Courier* sold several hundred extra copies on the strength of the two-page feature. The subject of their attention, though still declining to do more than expose himself to any stray female who came within range, smartened himself up with a new tracksuit and a freshly painted hood. The police were given a target to see them through a sadly law abiding summer.

The police, in point of fact, went even further over the top in their coverage of the affair than the local paper, which did at least have the excuse of literary licence in reporting events. Policemen quartered the grounds day and night in ingenious disguises - spoiled only by their reliance on navy blue as a base colour, and the crackling radios that burst into life at the most inopportune moments. The ladies of the force showed more sartorial variance in their choice of disguise but, since their more noticeable male colleagues invariably followed them at a discreet distance, the result was the same. Their quarry remained as elusive and undetected as a latter day Scarlet Pimpernel. Though, as one offended women had commented after encountering him, "You'd think a man as big as *that* would stand out even in his clothes."

Melody, of course, wasn't to know that the publicity far outstripped the man. As two pairs of eyes stared into each other's depths for what seemed an eternity to Melody, she found that her parched mouth could manage no more than a dry croak of protest, when what she really wanted was to announce her terror loudly to the world.

How long they would have remained like that, and what would have been the final outcome when the spell was broken, neither party was ever to know. The sound of running footsteps along the path from which her assailant had erupted stirred him to action once again. He bundled Melody roughly to one side and leaped for the wall as Len Saunders arrived just a moment too late. Hauling himself to the top with strength born of panic, the hooded figure dropped to the safety of the road on the other side.

"Sod it." Len doubled over, with his back against a yew tree, fighting desperately for his breath. "Lost the bastard again. How he can run and jump like that in the state he's in is beyond me. He didn't hurt you, did he?"

Melody had tried to stand up and discovered her legs strangely reluctant to support her. "No. He crashed into me, and knocked me over, but that was all. He was too intent on getting away from you to have time to do anything else."

"Lucky for you he was. You shouldn't be out here on your own whilst he's about. He just jumped out at a woman down by the lake. Didn't you hear her screaming?"

"No. I was too deep in my own thoughts to notice anything until he ran into me. Did he hurt the woman?"

"No. Luckily for her I was changing the times on the gates just beyond, and was across there like a shot. You should have seen the toe-rag run when he saw me bearing down on him." He sighed. "Oh well, I suppose I'd better go and ring the police. Bloody typical of them. Most days you can't move in here for the buggers, but today there isn't *one* of them to be had." He started to move away, then checked himself. "Tell you what though. Do you think you can go and telephone, whilst I go back and secure the woman? They have a nasty habit of melting away into the crowd after seeing our flasher. Too embarrassed to want to do anything about it I suppose."

5

Carol was coming back from her dinnertime excursion as Melody made her way to the telephone to report. She still carried the mask in the plastic carrier bag, but she could have saved herself the trouble of purloining it, because it hadn't been required. Tom had arrived late for their meeting, breathless and without explanation. He had shown very little interest in the mask, and none at all in having sex with her. Carol recognised that she would definitely have to procure the rubber apron if she wasn't to lose him.

6

Len made his way back to the nursery yard to report to Simon - having failed to find any trace of the flasher's victim when he returned to interview her. As he passed the Benedict Road entrance another man in park attendant's uniform was just coming in.

"Where have you been?" There was something about Dave Croftman, whose dark looks and black wavy hair gave him the appearance of an Italian Mafiosi, that Len didn't trust.

"Popped out for fags. Heavy night last night; I hadn't enough to see me through."

"And before that?" Len persisted.

"Patrolling in the woods. Why?"

"Our flasher's been at it again. I chased him but he got away."

"Whereabouts was that?" Dave selected a cigarette for himself, and offered one to Len, which he refused.

"In the woods." Len replied laconically as he walked off.

CHAPTER FOUR

Councillor Warren Hescott, leaning back comfortably in his soft leather chair, considered the meeting of the Middleton Leisure Services Ideas Committee reflectively.

The councillor was feeling liverish and it was making him even more irritable than usual. He studied his companions critically, wondering, not for the first time, what in God's name had ever inspired him to dream up such a damned fool scheme as an Ideas Committee in the first place?

It wasn't as if there was an idea amongst them worth discussing. Not in Councillor Hescott's opinion anyway. The air was full of talk of on-going situations and maximising assets, but nobody was actually saying anything – not in any language the old man understood anyway. His mind, as it was prone to of late, slipped easily away to a time when a younger and stronger Warren Hescott was first elected to the local council during the mid-1950's.

It had been a calculated assessment on Hescott's part to avoid membership of any of the larger political parties and remain independent. He had always preferred to be his own man; living his life as his conscience dictated. He didn't intend to enter a career where his actions would be governed by party policy, rather than by his own sense of right or wrong.

The decision, as it turned out, had brought Hescott more power than he would ever have known had he accepted the colours of one of the main runners. Local government in Middleton was finely divided between left and right and it frequently fell to Warren to enjoy the casting vote on a sensitive issue.

The councillor liked that. He was a man who enjoyed power for its own sake. He had done so as he built the local empire of hardware stores, which had gained him recognition after the war, and continued to do so throughout those early halcyon days in local politics. He had later added to that power by becoming chairman of the newly formed Leisure Services Committee as the result of a deal he had done with the ruling Tory party. Wheeling and dealing, playing one party off against another, Hescott had been a power in Middleton politics for all of....

"Good God!" He blinked in disbelief as it suddenly came to him just how long he *had* been in control.

"Councillor?" Lancelot Meadows, the weasel-like Assistant Director (Libraries) at his side, looked round in surprise.

Councillor Hescott frowned. He hadn't intended to speak out loud but, having done so, it seemed explanations would have to be forthcoming. It was fortunate that no one besides Meadows had heard his involuntary exclamation. He had no wish to bring it to the attention of the entire meeting just how long he had served. Someone might start to wonder if it wasn't, perhaps, time for a change?

"A milestone." Meadows trod warily when the explanation had been given. One never knew quite which way the contrary old sod beside him was going to leap next. It was his reputation for being bloody-minded which had kept him in power through successive changes of government. The public knew that with Hescott on their side they stood an even chance whatever the odds. The party with the majority at any given moment always considered him a sleeping tiger best left alone. It was little wonder that the Assistant Director (Libraries) had no wish to risk giving offence by speaking to him out of turn

"A silver jubilee." Hescott's mind wandered off to reflect on the two royal examples of the occasion, which had been celebrated during his lifetime.

Lancelot smiled as he suddenly understood, or thought he understood, what the other man was driving at. "You think that a small commemoration of some sort might be in order?" He ventured.

"Good Lord no!" The councillor was genuinely shocked at the suggestion. "I doubt if anyone will even notice. There's no one left from the early days, and none of the young whippersnappers running the show now will have an inkling. I wouldn't really want them to. Makes me feel old to think of it myself. Must make me seem some sort of Methuselah to the likes of Potter."

Meadows, nearing retirement himself, was able to smile at this sideswipe at the Director of Leisure Services, who had yet to see forty. Nevertheless, he took the opportunity later in the meeting to pass on to his chief the gist of his conversation with Hescott, as he understood it.

"Twenty five years eh?" Potter was a Glasgow Scot with the accent and attitudes of the back streets still heavily about him. "And ye ken he expects some sort of gesture on our part because of it?"

"I'm sure Councillor Hescott doesn't seek recognition for his years of service." Meadows had no love at all for the superior he considered to be little more than a blustering bully. "He simply mentioned the anniversary to me in passing, and now I've mentioned it to you. Whether or not you feel it demands some sort of commemoration is entirely up to you."

"He expects something big." Potter spoke directly to Wilson, the Parks Maintenance Co-ordinator. Gormann, the Assistant Director (Parks), was away on an evangelical mission in the north, so one link in the chain of command had to be by-passed. "Meadows tells me he'll no be too happy if we overlook it. I'm thinking you'd best sort something in record time."

Wilson was fully aware of the consequences for him if he offended Hescott and, through him, Potter as well. It was an unpleasant thought and, faced with it, his mind froze and refused to come up with a solution. This was something that had been happening to him more and more of late. His doctor had told him that it was a result of stress and would get worse if he didn't distance himself from the cause of it. Wilson was well aware that the cause was a job, with which he was unable to cope, but there was only one solution to a problem like that, and he baulked at even contemplating it.

He had made it to his present senior position and there was no going back from it now, thereby announcing to the world that he was unable to cope. Not with HP instalments on the dishwasher and the video still to be paid, quite apart from the deposit for the cottage he was hoping to buy in Yorkshire. Wilson liked Yorkshire - and so did his wife. She would be sure to make life hell for him if he put the cottage in jeopardy. And his children would lose the respect for him he fondly imagined they felt. Wilson didn't think he could face losing so much just because of an occasional trick of his mind. It would clear up in time he was sure, and then the headaches would fade away too. Nevertheless, he took a chance on this occasion, and voiced his uncertainty to Potter.

"That's your bother." Came back the uncompromising reply. "You're paid to manage the parks, so manage them. Just see to it that you do enough to get me that extra cash I'm wanting voted through at the next committee. I'd no want to be in your shoes if you bugger up all the grovelling I've been doing these past months."

Wilson turned away thoughtfully and sought the advice of John Death, the Parks Maintenance Manager (South), who was his immediate subordinate.

Death was a newcomer to the department, thrown up by the fourth of the reorganisations there had been since Potter had taken control. Each one brought about by the inefficiency of the staff he had inherited from the previous regime. Or so he would have the world believe.

He had done his best to rid himself of this chaff by constant purges and transfers to far-flung corners of the borough, rather in the fashion of those carried out during the latter days of Stalinist Russia. And he had been successful in his intent. Of the officer staff he had inherited only a handful of thick-skinned individuals remained.

It was a state of affairs beginning to rebound on the man now, however, robbing him, as it did, of his excuse for the continued lack of direction the department displayed. John Death was the third Parks Maintenance Manager (South) in as many years and, from the point of view of the parks and gardens under his control, was probably the worst.

Death was an opportunist who had recognised that where his predecessors went wrong was in making no immediate impact on the environment. Potter wanted to see results. 'Environmental improvements,' as he styled them. Good or bad, he wanted to be able to say, 'This is what has been done since I arrived here,' and dare anyone to criticise in any way.

John Death had many ideas with which to attract the Director's attention. Most involved such a shuffling of staff and movement of materials and machines that his parks were in a constant state of flux. No one dared develop the empathy with their workplace, which is the trademark of the gardener, because no one could be certain where they would be working week by week, or even what plants would be left there to tend.

The scheme by which the parks division sold off surplus plants to the public at reduced prices was John Death's latest. Surplus, under his interpretation of it, meaning anything the public were prepared to buy. Shrubs and bedding plants intended for beds and borders in the public domain were sold off at knockdown prices; first rate public relations, as Potter was quick to point out. What he overlooked in the euphoria of the moment, however, was that labour charges for that same weekend sale were in the order of three times the amount of money taken at the tills. What he didn't see was the depletion of the bedding in Death's (South) area that summer; the plants intended for it having formed the backbone of the sale.

Simon Spaulding, Area Supervisor of Middleton Hall since the reorganisation before the one which had brought John Death to Middleton, had begun by watching the machinations of his new manager with cynical resignation. It had quickly become disapproval, and then outright opposition, when the man turned his attention to the grounds of the Hall.

Now a state of affairs existed between them that couldn't really be dignified as war. Simon was sure Death saw him as no more than an irritation. A fly he allowed the freedom to buzz around, knowing full well that he could swat it any time he chose.

And buzz Simon did, as by move and counter move he managed to block the majority of the changes John Death sought to introduce to the Hall. It was a dangerous business, however, and Simon was fully aware that he had only to put a foot wrong to plunge from the tightrope he was walking to the hard earth below.

"Twenty five years," Death repeated thoughtfully, as his mind clicked into action at the scent of a fresh opportunity to sell himself as an ideas man. "So you want a big show put on?"

"According to the chief, he's expecting it. What do you think?"

"Something silver. Tree planting ceremonies generally go down well. What about a birch?"

Wilson, a little disappointed by his subordinate's lack of originality, couldn't help but show it. He had hoped to go back to Potter with something more than this. "I should have thought we'd already got more than enough birches around the borough. We seemed to plant forests of them to honour the Queen in '77."

"You can never have too many birches," the maintenance manager contradicted reproachfully. "The public love them."

"Perhaps," Wilson remained unconvinced, "but I was looking for something a little more out of the ordinary than that."

"What about an Atlas Cedar?" Simon Spaulding had been invited to the meeting as a token member of the supervisory staff. Listening to the conversation between his two immediate bosses had been a means of staving off the sleep that boredom, and the unaccustomed recycled air of the warm and windowless room, was dragging down on him. Not an indication of any real interest.

"Hardly silver." Death commented shortly.

"*Argentea*?" Simon persisted.

"Grey." The other summed it up critically

"What's silver about a birch besides its name?"

"I think Simon has a point there." Wilson broke in as his companions girded themselves for battle. "The occasion certainly calls for something a little less ordinary than a birch. If we were to purchase a cedar, it would not only serve its purpose as far as the councillor is concerned, but could be planted at Middleton Hall to replace the one Mr Sharpe's always bitching about us having felled. That way we satisfy two contrary old devils in one go. A good idea Simon," he smiled briefly at the younger of the men. "I can leave it with you then John?" He turned back to the other.

"If that's your choice?" Death pulled a face to emphasise the point that it certainly wasn't *his*. "And if we can purchase a suitable specimen at such short notice, of course."

"Try John. Try. I've never known you to fail in anything yet." Wilson patted his subordinate's shoulder encouragingly. "It looks as if the chief is winding up the meeting," his persuasive tones were suddenly clouded by anxiety, "I must get word to Hescott and tell him what's afoot. I'll say good day to you gentlemen."

"Good day," Simon replied politely, rising from his seat.

"*Argentea!*" Death snorted derisively, remaining firmly in his.

CHAPTER FIVE

Midnight was a lonely place. A vast auditorium in which the problems of the day were amplified into the Medusa of insomnia. Assailed by such a sleepless state, John Death lay listening to the regular breathing of his wife in the bed opposite with a mixture of jealousy and disapproval, as he relived the build-up to the problem weighing so heavily on his mind.

"John," Gerald Wilson had started this most uncomfortable period of Death's career just after coffee break that morning. "I've got Councillor Hescott on the telephone. He wants to confirm the tree planting next month."

"It's all in hand Gerald. No problem this end." Arrested in the act of filling his pipe, Death replied with easy urbanity.

Wilson frowned. He was not a smoker himself and considered the habit offensive in others. His silent disapproval of the clouds of smoke to which his subordinate subjected him every day was close to breaking point, and he welcomed an opportunity to take Death to task for whatever reason. "He seemed to be under the impression that the tree to be planted was a birch."

The maintenance manager weighed his words carefully before answering. "I did write to Hescott to that effect Gerald," he admitted.

"But we agreed a cedar John." The tone of sweet reason was belied by the glint in Wilson's eyes.

"Did we?" Death managed to sound genuinely surprised. "Wasn't that just an idea of Spaulding's? A bit outlandish I thought."

"A pretty sound idea *I* thought," the other countered with unusual force. "And so does Councillor Hescott now I've put it to him."

"You've overruled me?" Death enquired heavily.

"Better than you overruling me, I think," Wilson replied pointedly. "Now perhaps you'll have a word with the councillor about it." He held out the telephone receiver.

"John Death here, councillor," the parks manager accepted it reluctantly, and addressed himself into the mouthpiece. "I understand there's some sort of confusion over the choice of tree for your commemoration?"

"Seems to me that the only one confused is you." Came the blunt reply. "What's the idea of trying to palm me off with a birch? Mr Wilson tells me I'm supposed to have a cedar."

Death swallowed his antagonism as best he could. Why *did* everyone constantly disagree with him? "I'm sorry Councillor Hescott. I was exercising my discretion in the matter. I thought a birch would fit the bill."

"Weren't there rather a lot of birches planted in '77?"

"It's my opinion that you can never have too many birches, councillor." Death wheeled out his oft-repeated tome.

"Well I'm afraid I don't share it. There are more than enough planted around the borough already I should say. One more or less wouldn't even be noticed. No. If I'm to suffer a tree planting ceremony it has to be a tree worth planting. I like the idea of the cedar. Damn it - I want something that will outlast me - and there's no guarantee that a birch will do that. Short-lived rubbish, so I'm told."

"I understand your feelings completely, councillor." Death adopted his most conciliatory tone. "But there is more to it than that I'm afraid. I weighed the matter up carefully before coming to a decision, I can assure you. The simple fact of the matter is that it all boils down to availability of finance and availability of stock.

We're on a very tight budget at the moment, as you know. That limits the amount we can afford to pay for a tree. A cedar at the sort of price we're talking of would be a very small subject. *Very* small. It might tend to reduce the ceremony to its own stature. A birch would be a different matter entirely. We have several of a suitable size already in the nursery that would cost us nothing. I really think you ought to give it a little more consideration, you know."

"Don't try to teach me to suck eggs Mr Death. I was chairing the Leisure Services Committee when you were still in short trousers. I know all the ways of getting finances through for pet projects. I invented a lot of them myself. If you want money to buy a tree you can find it easily enough. And don't try to palm me off with that rubbish about availability," Death had made a sound suggestive of interruption, "I can even help you with that. Try looking in Gordon's garden. You'll find a perfect specimen, container grown, and just the variety we're talking of." There was silence at the other end of the telephone. "Well?" Hescott prompted.

Death found his voice with great difficulty. "I can't take a tree from Mr Gordon's garden without his agreement." He got out at last.

"Why not? He put it in there without the borough's agreement. It was the last one needed to complete the Royal Avenue, and he hid it out of pure bloody mindedness because he didn't get the top job when we amalgamated in '63. I'd forgotten all about the thing until I went to their garden party last year. Ostentatious tomfoolery that was. Typical Gordon! The tree was there though. Just as I'd always suspected. Hidden behind his chicken house, but grown too tall to be out of sight anymore. Much too big for his garden. You'll be doing him a favour when you take it away."

"Councillor Hescott, even if you do suspect Mr Gordon of hiding a tree to which he has no right, there's nothing I can do about it now. You're talking of twenty years ago. It would be a very difficult charge to prove."

Snort from Hescott. "Who's asking you to prove anything? I didn't say you should take the man to court about it. I simply suggested that, as he took the tree from us in the first place, you have a perfect right to take it back."

"And if he disputes ownership? It just might be a tree he purchased legitimately."

Second snort, louder than the first. "Don't prevaricate man. That tree was stolen from the Parks Department twenty years ago, and it's the tree I want planted in my name now. I don't want a birch. I don't even want a different cedar. I want the tree from Gordon's garden - or there will be no ceremony in August. And no further assistance from me in pushing through Mr Potter's development scheme. Do I make myself clear?"

"Perfectly clear councillor."

"Good."

The ringing of the bell as the receiver was replaced at the other end of the line had sounded a knell in Death's ears. The memory of it still echoed in his mind as he searched fruitlessly for sleep.

2

Arnold Lovett also had a problem that prevented him sleeping, but for a very different reason. The native tribes of North America were said to cease hostilities at sunset for fear that the spirits of their slain would find it impossible to make their way to the land of the dead in the dark. Arnold, not prepared to follow their example, was taking the battle to the enemy in the dead of night.

If only Len Saunders had been looking out of the window of his lodge in the early hours of that morning he would have had the opportunity to settle things once and for all by dealing with his adversary away from prying eyes. Like all god-fearing park attendants, however, the man was sound asleep, and never to know what an opportunity he missed. With his spade over his shoulder, and a swagger in his walk, the treasure seeker made his way openly along the main drive of the Hall.

There were some people who might have been afraid to find themselves adrift in the night time park, with the light from the high riding moon making devils of wind-blown branches and ambuscades of darker patches of shadow, but Arnold was devoid of fear. Saunders would have dismissed him as being too thick to suffer nerves, but the truth was kinder to the man. Arnold would dare anything to achieve a purpose once his mind was set on it. It was the spirit that had built an empire, and it was going to win the prize Arnold so resolutely sought.

Giving a wide berth to the lodge where Wilson lived, Arnold made his way towards his goal. The soil Len had replaced a few days before was loose, and the excavation of the site to the depth where his previous efforts had been interrupted was the work of moments for Arnold. Cut, press and lift. Cut, press and lift. The digging had achieved a steady rhythm when the downward stroke of the spade was arrested by something that jarred every bone in Arnold's body when he struck it. In a fever of anticipation he dropped to his knees, regretting after all that he hadn't troubled to bring a torch with him, and that the hole was too deep for the light from the moon to illuminate its base.

The obstacle in the hole was cold and rough to the touch. So suggestive of a stone slab that it could be nothing else. Arnold's scrabbling fingers sought an edge to it as the excitement rising inside him set his heart racing wildly.

There *was* an edge. The trembling man straddled the hole, slipped as many fingers as he could manage under the slab, and lifted with straining shoulders. The stone moved easily, and in a moment Arnold was reaching into the further depths below it to encounter a wooden box, which weighed hopefully heavy, as he hefted it to the surface.

3

Several hours later Simon stood gazing thoughtfully into the hole, which had so unexpectedly reappeared in the middle of the lawn.

Len Saunders was on late turn that week, so it was afternoon before Simon was able to speak to the park attendant about the troubling discovery he had made.

"You *did* fill in the hole the last time?" Simon asked, having distracted the other man from his task of oiling a faulty lock on the tennis courts gate.

"You know I did." Len took the opportunity to roll himself a cigarette.

"I know *someone* did. I wanted to get it clear whether it was you or Dave."

"That lazy bugger! You'd be as likely to see George Rioden filling it in. Why do you ask?"

"Because it reappeared this morning, complete with Joe Grubb's missing toolbox and old Gordon's missing cockerel in an advanced state of decay."

Len's eyes gleamed. "The bastard wanted a cockerel, so I made him a present of one. Nothing wrong with *that* was there?"

There was no answering smile on the supervisor's face. "Gordon might think so."

"I doubt it. He was always complaining what a vicious blighter the thing was, and how he wished he had the stomach to wring its neck. It wasn't me did him a favour by killing it, though. A fox had done that. I just found the body in the woods where the fox had left it." A cherubic smile wreathed the attendant's face. "It must have been well rotten by now. I bet he got the stink of it all over him."

"He probably did." Simon replied soberly. "So has Joe's toolbox. You didn't have to use that did you? You knew how much it meant to him."

"I know he was a bloody nuisance, always chuntering on about it when people were trying to talk about other things. Here…" Len's eyes narrowed suddenly, "are you trying to give me a rollicking?"

"I'm trying to point out to you that I expect my senior attendant to show a sight more responsibility."

"Well sod you then." He turned his back and began pulling noisily at the lock and chain.

Simon shrugged his shoulders and walked away. At the nursery yard he found Peter Gilray waiting for him.

"Is that aimed at me?" The latter demanded brusquely, pointing to something posted on the staff notice board outside the men's mess room.

Simon walked across to it and read:

It has been brought to the notice of the Director of Leisure Services that certain members of staff are bringing animals to work with them.

It is to be understood that this practice is completely unacceptable and must cease from this date.

Staff found guilty of defying the ban will leave themselves open to the sternest disciplinary proceedings.

John Death. Parks Manager.

"He did ask if Sammy belonged to you." Simon admitted.

"And you told him?"

"I told him he didn't, but you know what Death's like once he gets an idea into his head. He probably thinks I was just covering for you."

"Bastard," the gardener muttered. "Still," he brightened suddenly. "Death can believe what he likes. Sammy *isn't* mine. Can't help it if he follows me about can I?"

As if to emphasise the point, the two men were joined by the ragged animal, which ambled out of the mess room, and stood looking up at Peter with adoring eyes.

"Nearly had the postman again this morning." Peter grinned at the memory. "Came cycling past the cascade when I was weeding there before tea. Old Sam was over the fence and after him like a shot. I've never seen anyone pedal so fast. His feet were a blur. Then for afters Sam chased a jogger all the way back. He hadn't looked as if he could even walk up the slope until he had his heels nipped, but then...Oh Christ! Here's trouble."

A well known car was nosing into the yard behind Simon, who glanced round to establish that it was his superior. He turned back to Peter, but he had disappeared. Unfortunately, however, he had omitted to take the dog with him in his flight.

Mr Death sat in his car looking meaningly from Simon to Sam and back again. "You've seen my ruling about animals?" He enquired coldly when he had eventually joined the younger man.

"Yes," Simon admitted.

"And?"

"I was just showing it to Sammy."

A sadder and wiser Simon, now fully aware of his manager's total lack of sympathy towards him, emerged from his office a little while later, after a private conversation with Mr Death, and went in search of someone to blame.

Carol, with troubles of her own, had intended to approach Simon about borrowing the rubber apron, but one glance at his face warned her of the futility of her mission, and forced the postponement of the request to a more amenable moment.

Peter, very wisely, took himself off to the opposite side of the grounds, with Sammy the dog happily trotting at his heels and snapping at passing schoolchildren.

Maggot smiled sagely, and thought to himself that if Simon's days in charge really were numbered, the bosses couldn't make the mistake of overlooking Joseph Grubb a second time.

Only Melody, genuinely sorry that Simon should find himself in trouble, risked a sympathetic smile as he passed.

With feelings too deep for words, Simon made his way past them all without a sign.

CHAPTER SIX

"Carol's been behaving very strangely lately," Melody observed to Simon, as she stood looking out across dark waters alive with an inner turbulence that matched her own.

"Has she?" Simon was leaning against the guard rail with his back to the river. His eyes swept aimlessly along the upper ramifications of the vast Wisteria, which dominated the front of 'Cricket House'. The mansion, once the property of Sir Richard Greenward, late of the foreign office during the last socialist government, was rumoured to have been purchased on behalf of an Arab consortium wishing to be conveniently situated for both motorway and airport. He answered automatically, his mind off considering the passage from *'Julius Caesar'* describing, 'the tide in the affairs of man which, taken at the flood, leads on to fortune,' and wondering if by any stretch of the imagination it could be taken as applying to the situation facing him now.

He had been surprised when Melody suggested they spend their lunchtime walking by the river. Admittedly the invitation came after Simon had been outlining the history of Middleton, which had developed from a small hamlet discovered by city dwellers rich enough to build a second home there. He had spiced the account with racy stories of Dick Turpin's exploits in the area, and those of a certain local squire, who had kept his three mistresses in adjoining houses during the eighteenth century. It was possible that Melody had simply wanted to see the places of which she had been told, but, nevertheless, Simon was wary.

It wasn't just the moral obligation he always felt not to become involved with any of the staff for whom he was responsible. Nor any feelings he had for the dark-haired woman who shared the more intimate moments of his life. There was something beyond the pretty face looking up at his so attentively that hinted at more than Melody was

44

prepared to tell him. An emotional undercurrent capable of dragging the unwary down with her and carrying them away.

"What's she been doing?" Simon studied his companion carefully from the corner of his eye, abandoning the beauty of blue panicles of wisteria in its second flush of flower.

Unobserved by his subjects, Maggot studied the two people leaning against the riverside rail, taking careful note of their proximity to each other, and the manner in which the girl constantly looked up into the face of the man. He had just emerged from the 'Fisherman's Rest' where he had been indulging in a little premature celebration of the good fortune he was about to enjoy. Mr Death hadn't promised in so many words, but he had hinted strongly that promotion could be on the cards for Maggot in the near future, and that could only mean that the usurper Spaulding would soon be gone. The maintenance manager enjoyed staff around him who were unquestioningly loyal and that Maggot was prepared to be, so long as such loyalty gained its proper recognition and reward. Simon, on the other hand, always remained his own man whatever happened. A quirk of character that made him as dangerous to Maggot as he was to Death. With all these qualifying considerations to the forefront of his mind, Maggot watched through jaundiced eyes as the situation developed.

"Hoping to get his end away." He reported later to an interested mess room.

"And why not?" Henry Hatherway, the park's tractor driver, enquired indulgently. "There's no law against it so long as they're both willing."

"But it ain't right." Maggot spat out his words spitefully. "Sexual harassment, that's what it is."

"Did Melody look harassed?"

"That ain't the point. Management ain't supposed to take advantage of the workers that way. It's not a natural way of carrying on."

"I'd agree with you if he was trying it on with you or me," Henry exchanged a secret wink with Tom Hollins in the corner. "That wouldn't be natural at all. But to try it on with Melody seems completely natural to me."

"You tried it on with her, didn't you?" Jack Higgins looked up innocently from the book he was reading. "Was that natural?"

"I never did!" Maggot was beginning to regret having raised the subject amongst such an unsympathetic group of people. "Anyone who says so is a liar."

"Carol must have got it wrong then." Higgins nodded sagely. "She must have misheard what you were saying to the girl. I must admit that I never believed it. I've always thought you were gay."

"What do you mean?" Maggot caught the broad smile passing from face to face around the mess room and realised at last that he was being made the butt of their humour. "Clever bastards ain't you?" He snarled. "Well you have your laugh whilst you can. My time's coming. Let's see who's laughing then."

"Do you think he knows something we don't?" Hollins nodded after the retreating Maggot as the last echoes of the door slamming died.

"All mouth and trousers. Maggot always was." Henry remarked unkindly.

"Simon was in the shit about Sammy though." Hollins persisted. "Peter says that Death bollocked the hell out of him about it. It's a pity. I like Simon. Give Death a reason to move him though and I don't reckon we'd see him for dust. Then who knows? We just might have Maggot in charge."

"Never likely to happen." Higgins turned back to his book. "Not even Death would be daft enough to put

Maggot over us - whatever he does with Simon. One governor is pretty much the same as another most of the time…but Maggot…" He withdrew back into the story he was reading and silence settled once more.

2

The object of their interest was still no nearer discovering what was on Melody's mind, and he was becoming a little impatient with the girl in consequence.

"Time we were making our way back," he glanced at the clock on the tower above the brewery and then checked his watch for confirmation.

"Oh," Melody commented wretchedly, "is it already as late as that?"

"Twenty to. It'll take about ten minutes from here."

"Okay." Melody had been aware for some time that her continued silence was costing her the sympathy of her companion. She wasn't surprised. Her relationships with men always floundered on an inability to communicate. Somehow she had hoped that Simon might prove in some way easier to talk to - it being so important to her that she did just that – but, in the event, he had turned out to be no different from the rest.

Not that she was blaming Simon for her dilemma as she trailed along wretchedly in his wake. She knew he must be wondering why she had bothered to suggest an outing in the first place, and at least he hadn't tried anything on. Most men were intent on making every relationship as physical as possible. Accepting with bad grace the knowledge that Melody truly offered total refusal when she said 'no'. Muriel Bainbridge's advice about consenting adults might have been enough to put Carol's mind at rest, but it couldn't do the same for Melody. An insurmountable barrier stood between her and anything more than a purely platonic relationship with a man. Melody was a boy.

Gary Norman Carnforth she had been christened in the parish church at Bledstock in Cumbria. The eventual triumph for middle-aged parents who had consistently failed to conceive. His early life had given no warning of the sorrow he was destined to bring down on such undeserving but (in the case of his mother at least) forgiving heads.

The young Gary did display a certain preference for more gentle pursuits than his peers, and he favoured the company of girls rather than boys, but there was nothing tangible about him at which to point a finger. At least, not until he grew older, and girlfriends remained just that - girls who were his friends and nothing more.

Even so, he led a blameless life, and the fears which tormented him through so many sleepless nights were bottled up so tightly their existence could be denied. Gary had no real friends among the boys of the town, and the one or two he found distressingly attractive he avoided; fearing the names he might be called if his secret liking for them was accidentally revealed; well aware by now that he was trapped inside a body with which he had nothing in common.

Gary's father disowned him when a spark of misplaced honesty caused him to reveal his predicament to his uncomprehending parents one tearful Friday soon after his seventeenth birthday. His mother tried desperately to understand, but in the end found it impossible to cope with the revelation that the child she had suffered so much to give birth to was a changeling; a freak; a cruel joke of nature. Realising how much he had hurt them, and that there was no way now in which his secret could remain safe, Gary accepted the painful inevitability of his departure from the village he had known all his life.

His exit, when he made it, was unrehearsed, and as unexpected to him as it was to his parents. The decision came between leaving home and arriving at the office one morning. Checking his pockets, and finding he had enough money to get by, he telephoned his mother from the station and told her what he intended to do.

Gary's mother cried, but she made no plea to him to change his mind. Mary Carnforth was a realist and she could see that her son's decision was best for everyone. She asked him to keep in touch, but that was all. With a jump of his heart Gary realised he was free at last of all the hypocrisies and restraints of his former existence. Away from Bledstock he would be able to express himself in whatever way he chose.

His initial move was to give himself over completely to his adopted sex and abandon the deception of continuing as a man. This was easy enough to accomplish, requiring only the purchase of women's clothing at a large department store.

He chose clothes to camouflage rather than attract. Gary had never had the problem of facial hair, so the physical discrepancies between what he was and what he pretended to be were of little account. His voice was, perhaps, a tone too deep, but that aside Gary was to all intents and purposes a woman at last.

The next morning he donned his male identity for the last time and, having checked out of the hotel, made his way to a discreet part of the local common. There he changed out of his old clothes, leaving both them and Gary abandoned in the undergrowth. That evening Melody Carnforth checked into a different hotel.

The next few months, spent in establishing a new life for herself, proved to be the hardest part of all. Achieving the physical appearance of a woman had been unbelievably easy; maintaining the role well enough to gain employment no harder - though there was a little unpleasantness about a missing P60. It was the emotional readjustment Melody had to make that proved crippling to her already damaged psyche.

Men went out of their way to approach her now and it was often difficult to remain aloof to their advances, even though she knew it would be fatal to succumb.

It was equally hard to forge a close friendship with any of the girls she now came into contact with. How could she join in discussions about boyfriends and babies - their two main topics of conversation? She was always afraid she might accidentally say or do something that would reveal her secret, laying it bare to a sniggering world.

Fear of discovery was constantly with the girl, and yet it contrasted strangely with the choice of name to go with her new identity. To call herself Marie or Rachel might have been more natural and unobtrusive, but she had chosen Melody as an act of deliberate defiance. She wanted to be able to confront the world and say, "It's not my fault I'm different. Accept me as I am, because there's no way I can change," but that she dare not do. Instead, she sent her name on ahead as emissary, hoping that through it someone might notice and understand.

No one did, though Billy Danton had come close before the pressure of their living together got too much for him to handle. Theirs had been a relationship of total innocence, yet when Melody looked back on it after Billy had abandoned her, much as she had earlier abandoned her parents; a sense of guilt tainted the memory of the life they had shared.

For a while after they split up Melody came closer to total despair than at any other period in her life. She started to drift dangerously, becoming involved in the seamier side of big city living. It was her inherent common sense which saved her, drawing her back from the abyss into which she was sliding, to begin the slow recovery that eventually led to Middleton Hall, and her present dilemma.

The first six months of Melody's employment were almost over. With the completion of this probationary period would come the need for a medical examination to allow her to be considered for superannuation and sick pay. Afraid of how her employers would react to the revelation of her true sex, Melody had steeled herself to tell the more sympathetic Simon first, and see how he reacted. Her nerve had failed her at the last moment, however, and so she followed Simon disconsolately as they made their way back to the nursery. She was afraid now that not only was she no nearer knowing what might befall her at the hands of the council doctor, but she had also succeeded in alienating Simon at the very time when she might need his help the most.

CHAPTER SEVEN

The dawn that greeted the following morning was bright and seemed set fair with the promise of continuing good weather. The sun, rising above the tabletop heads of the trees comprising the great Cedar avenue to the rear of the Hall, reflected on myriad spider's webs hanging heavy with dew. Simon, out early to absorb the beauty of a day too young as yet to be spoiled by problems, found his eyes attracted by a movement in one of the Cedars. A heron, rising from the uppermost branches of the tree, was flapping lazily away in the direction of the river. Savouring the regal splendour of the great bird Simon walked on, his eyes following the track it had taken across the sky. So intently, in fact, that he all but stumbled over a mallard duck crossing the lawn ahead of him, guiding her following brood with soft, caressing calls far removed from her usual sharp quack.

It was a day to feel at peace with the world and Simon was prepared to do just that. Not even the knowledge that John Death was savouring the same pleasures as he enjoyed would have been enough to dispel Simon's sense of bonhomie, though he might have been surprised to know that his manager was there. Death, however, was keeping out of sight. He was parked in a lay-by opposite the main entrance to the grounds, logging the arrival of each member of staff. Seeking ammunition with which to rid himself of his turbulent supervisor, he was checking that Simon was not allowing latecomers to escape unpunished.

Sitting alert with pen poised to record names and times had been fine at first, but arrivals were, necessarily, few and far between. The excitement of the chase was beginning to pall for the silent watcher. His eyelids, which had grown heavy some time ago, kept trying to close. He turned on the car radio and, in an effort to combat sleepiness, tuned into a news channel. Death was a man who prided himself on keeping abreast of world events. He could talk for hours on the changing nuance of international politics; much to the chagrin of his wife, who found the subject dull and intolerably boring.

Dave Croftman was on early turn that morning and his name was ticked off as he strolled past John Death without noticing him there. The attendant was also interested in keeping abreast of the news, but his was a more parochial interest. Something in the local paper he was studying amused Dave. He smiled broadly as he digested an account of the latest of a series of burglaries plaguing the homes of the wealthier residents of the streets surrounding the grounds of the Hall. Already Isaac Sharpe was leading his group into the fray. Demanding that the police take more positive action to combat the crime wave before citizens at risk were driven to adopt a united stance on their own behalf.

Croftman folded the paper and slipped it into his pocket as he reached the attendants' office just inside the park gates. Whistling a tune through his teeth, he armed himself with paper-picker and black PVC sack. Whatever it was that had interested him in the report of the robberies had certainly set him in a good humour for the day. He scooped up an abandoned hypodermic syringe and deposited it in his bag with a smile as he disappeared into the depths of the woodlands.

Melody, on the other hand, was feeling wretched as she made her way into work. Her outing with Simon the previous day had left her even more confused and unsure than before. The sleepless night, which followed, had gone nowhere towards helping her make up her mind what she ought to do. The simplest remedy, to postpone the problem by going sick before the fateful day, could be no more than a holding action. It might, however, give her time to reflect and decide on a definite move. She felt she had been right to shy away from revealing her secret to Simon, but at the same time experienced a deep regret that there was no one in her world she could trust enough to share the burden of her knowledge.

The realisation of this total lack of a confidante had increased Melody's sense of loneliness to the point where it dominated every aspect of her life. Waking or sleeping, it brooded in the dark corners of her existence like a living entity, unremittingly malignant. Not for the first time since she had fled Bledstock, Melody experienced a pang of homesickness and a longing to see her mother once again. It was this longing with which she was battling as she stumbled dejectedly past Death and vanished along the main drive of the Hall.

Sammy, the dog, sniffed thoughtfully at the door of the car parked in the lay-by. He recognised the scent on it as belonging to the angry human he had sensed to be inimical towards him. The angry human had snarled and directed other obviously provocative noises at the nice humans who petted him. Sammy looked carefully around. The scent was certainly strong but there was no sign of its owner. He lifted a hind leg and carefully marked the door of the car so that when the angry human returned he would know that he (Sammy) had been there and had observed his presence. That done, he scratched the ground with his hind legs and, with his tail awag, trotted on into the grounds in search of his trusted companion Peter.

Simon, meanwhile, had made his way by circuitous paths to Pharaoh's Walk, which cut deep into one of the areas of woodland with which the grounds were dotted. A wall built of very old and very weathered brick lay back from the path. It was almost hidden by one of the parallel lines of tall Yew hedges planted to direct the eye towards a statue standing alone in a glade at the end of the walk. He hauled himself up onto the wall with a grunt, looking out across the grass enclosure towards numerous polythene tunnels in the nursery garden beyond. Something showing white amongst the green caught his eye. He dropped down from the wall to investigate.

Mushrooms. He had discovered mushrooms. A wealth of buttons pushing up through the basal mat of the unmown grass. Peeling off his jacket and forming it into a sling, Simon bent swiftly to gather as many as he could. The exquisite aroma caressed his senses as he worked. The supervisor had an almost insatiable appetite for mushrooms and would have picked more if the shrill call of a factory siren hadn't warned him it was time to begin the day's work. With a last regretful glance at the remaining fungi, Simon hurried off to add his name to the attendance register and set the day's work in motion.

It was some hours later when Len Saunders brought the tennis ticket returns to Simon's office as he sat lethargically checking bonus sheets, and planning the bacon and eggs with –possibly – tomatoes, which would accompany the mushrooms when he ate them later.

Relations between the two men had still not recovered from the affair of Mr Gordon's cockerel; such meetings as they had in the course of their respective duties being strained affairs marked by pregnant silence. Now Len stood staring at the mushrooms displayed in Simon's coat as it lay on top of the filing cabinet - its contents out of harm's way.

"What can I do for you Len?" Simon looked up from the stack of papers on his desk and endeavoured, without much success, to instil a degree of warmth into his greeting.

"I've brought the tennis returns." The other answered absently, his eyes still inclined towards the contents of Simon's jacket. "Pick those mushrooms in the park did you?"

"In the nursery garden," Simon flicked through the sheaf of papers Len had handed him. "There were quite a few, so I picked all I could carry. I love mushrooms."

"So do I." Len's tone was ominous. "I wondered where mine had gone to this morning."

"I'm sorry?" Simon looked up in surprise at the sharpness of the attendant's tone.

"Dave Croftman and me take it in turns to pick them. When he's on early turn he has them. When I am, I do. It's a perk of the job. Dave was on early turn this morning because I swapped with him for personal reasons, but we didn't swap our turns with the mushrooms. Today was my day for them just the same. I was a little later going out to pick them, that was all."

Simon's smile was a mistake. He admitted it to himself later. "And I got in first? Never mind Len. Have your turn tomorrow."

"Tomorrow's Dave's turn," the attendant commented brusquely.

"Then you'll just have to wait until the day after," Simon summed up the situation, responding irritably to Len's abrasive attitude, "because you're not getting any of these."

It was not the attitude to be adopted by a responsible supervisor. Even as he said it, Simon realised that. The devil was in him though, and he refused to learn. One morning, shortly after his confrontation with Simon, Len emerged from his lodge to discover punctures in both front and back tyres of his bike. Being obliged, as a result, to unlock the gates on foot, he reached the nursery garden very late in the morning to discover that Simon, out of pure bloody mindedness, had taken a turn with the mushrooms again.

It was Maggot who approached Simon this time, in his capacity as shop steward. Once more Simon should have known better, but his love life had soured. He and his lady had quarrelled bitterly two days earlier and when he had attempted to telephone her the previous evening to apologise for his lack of understanding there was no reply.

Tortured by half formed fears of where she might have been and what she might have been doing; Simon was in no mood for diplomacy. When Maggot placed the full weight of the union behind Len in his dispute with Simon, the complainant found himself given very short shrift.

Secretly delighted by the supervisor's response, Maggot pointed out that the next stage of the grievance procedure, as laid down by the borough council, was to put the matter before Mr Death for judgement. Simon's reply was brief and to the point. "Sod off and do it then." It was his only comment, and Maggot was happy to hurry off and oblige.

At this point a nervous tap on the office door heralded Carol, with a request that protective clothing be provided for her. By now in a mood to quarrel with anyone and everyone who came within his orbit, Simon accused her of constantly worrying him for things she had no need of, delivering a curt refusal to provide her with any further clothing that week.

The accusation struck home and Carol slunk off guiltily without offering any further argument, but Simon had overreached himself yet again. Carol's request had been legitimate on this occasion. There was eelworm in one of the glasshouses and the soil had to be drenched with insecticide.

John Death heard Maggot's list of complaints against Simon without betraying by word or expression that they sounded as sweet to him as they did to his informant.

Squabbling with park attendants, swearing at a shop steward and refusing a member of staff access to protective clothing, the provision of which was specified in the department's 'Safety Codes of Practice'. All solid foundation material for the case he was building for disciplinary proceedings to be taken against the district supervisor.

"Carol's always pestering me for clothing," Simon defended himself on one count at least. Albeit very half-heartedly.

"Then give it to her man. She can hardly misuse a rubber apron and respirator." With one sentence Death plumbed new depths in total ignorance of the motivations of his work force. "As for this other business. What are your attendants doing coming in at 6:30 in the first place? Starting time is an hour later everywhere else in the department."

"It's tradition." Simon explained, without any great hopes of retaining it as such now that it had been noticed.

"Then it's time that it wasn't." Came the uncompromising reply. "From tomorrow this park will fall into line with all the others and open an hour later in the mornings."

"We all know who's at the back of this," Len hissed vindictively, reading the latest memorandum to be posted on the ever-changing noticeboard.

Simon listened sadly, but had at last gained enough wisdom to ignore the accusation. Nor did he voice the sudden thought that at least they'd all have an equal chance at the mushrooms now.

In that, however, he was wrong. Alerted to their presence by the ramifications of the affair, Mr Gordon made a point of picking all the mushrooms he could find before the new opening time of the park. "Nectar of the Gods." He remarked to his wife as he watched her frying them for his breakfast. "Much too rich for council workers palates."

And of the council workers involved in the affray, perhaps Carol could be judged the one who gained the most. Next day she wore apron and boots openly as she left the nursery at dinner time with the respirator swinging jauntily on her arm. To her, at least, the mushrooms had revealed aphrodisiac qualities by greatly improving her love life.

CHAPTER EIGHT

A humour as black and deep as his previous mood had been ebullient lay heavily across Simon Spaulding as he surveyed the state of his life through jaundiced eyes. Just lately his world seemed to have settled on to a war footing, with fighting being carried out on so many fronts he was in danger of being overwhelmed.

There was no doubt in Simon's mind who was responsible for this state of affairs either. John Death had destroyed the spirit of the park, replacing it with an atmosphere of transience and mistrust. No one felt secure in their job anymore. No one felt permanent. Whilst there was no saying *when* the call would come and a transfer to a different district announced, there was no doubt that for most, if not all of the staff, the call would come sooner rather than later. Death was a man who believed settled staff to be idle staff and that he wouldn't tolerate.

It was why quarrels developed more easily than before. Some, like Maggot, were jockeying for power, hoping proof of their allegiance to the maintenance manager would lead to plum roles in the new order. Some, such as Simon or Len Saunders, cared enough about the grounds to be left frustrated and angry by the way in which maladministration was destroying their character, and the knowledge that too public a criticism of management policy would leave them as prime candidates for an early transfer themselves. Some, like Carol and Dave Croftman, were simply taking advantage of the department's gradual descent into chaos to further their own ends.

Croftman was seldom to be seen during the middle hours of the day anymore. When on early turn he would clean the toilets and empty the litter bins once the park was open, but that was all. Once the bare minimum of work was completed there was no finding him until mid-afternoon. Had Len Saunders been on speaking terms with Simon he might have mentioned the attendant's behaviour to him. Had Simon not been harassed in so many ways most of the time he might have noticed it for himself. As it was, if it crossed his mind at all that Croftman was not in evidence, he put it down to the size of the grounds, or the extraneous duties in other parks which the rundown of attendant coverage had created, turning his mind back to more important matters.

More important matters included the present state of his love life. Or, to be more accurate, his present lack of one. Until very recently Simon had been supremely content. Christine, his long-time lover, had been born under the sign of cancer the crab, however, and, true to her birth sign, considered her family to be of paramount importance in her life.

At first this caused no clash of interests between them. Christine had long ago lost touch with her husband, Barry, a long distance lorry driver who had failed to return from a European haul. It had come as no surprise to the woman to lose her husband in this way. She had long suspected him of being involved in smuggling of one sort or another, activities she considered a threat to the security of her family. The loss of her spouse had relieved the danger and Christine had settled down to devote her life to bringing up her three sons. Then Simon had arrived on the scene, somehow reawakening feelings within her she had thought irretrievably dead.

Christine, whilst enjoying the physical dimension Simon had restored to her emotional life, was inclined to resent her younger lover for reaching her so easily. In consequence, she spent much of her time erecting obstacles between them, which, with contrariness typical of her sex; she hoped and expected he would surmount in some way.

The latest obstacle, over which she and Simon had quarrelled so bitterly, however, seemed insurmountable. The errant Barry had re-emerged from her past, still her husband (Christine, though not a practising catholic, retained enough of her belief in the creed to refuse divorce under any circumstances) and wanting to pick up their relationship at the point where he had so suddenly broken it off.

She made no mention of Simon to her husband and swore her sons to secrecy on that score. They, seeing the return of their father as an opportunity to ease restrictive maternal bonds, readily agreed, and stood back to allow their parents to rejoin the broken ends of their marriage. Uneasily, and, as yet, unconsummated.

Simon, left out in the cold vastness of an emotional no man's land, was forced to adopt the role of observer, whilst praying that the marriage would waste no time in failing a second time.

2

Maggot, of course, knew nothing of the problems of his supervisor's private life. Had he done so, he would have cared even less. His thoughts and dreams revolved around the recognition of his qualities he was convinced was now only a matter of weeks away. With that in mind, he had begun to prepare himself for his forthcoming promotion by dressing more smartly to come to work, and even investing in the expense of a new trilby hat. His daydreams concerned themselves entirely with his stepping in to fill the vacancy when Simon was removed from office. Of Mr Death congratulating him on taking over with such a lack of fuss and carrying .out his duties so well. Of the rest of the garden staff treating him with a new respect as they recognised at last those qualities in his character, which they had overlooked before. Maggot dreamed relentlessly, and as he dreamed his ever-probing finger plumbed new depths in either nostril.

3

WPC Sarah Mackenzie, patrolling the grounds of the Hall, was even more ignorant than Maggot was on the subject of the undercurrents affecting the lives of the people responsible for maintaining them.

Sarah was one of the Home Beat officers for that part of Middleton in which the Hall was situated and had been facing the problems of real policing for all of six weeks since she had passed out from the police training college at Hendon.

It had been a less than eventful six weeks. Three people told the time, one lost child and six lost dogs found, twelve separate propositions, from male colleagues she was sharing a duty with, fended off successfully.

After three dogs, and five propositions, Sarah had stood back from herself to consider, dispassionately, whether she was, in some way, at fault for what had befallen her; none of which was why she had joined the force. An item of news in the *Courier* had already made Sarah certain of the reason for that. Fate had brought her to the district in order to apprehend the felon they had dubbed 'The Middleton Hall Rapist'.

Sarah Mackenzie had been born and grown up - not in the Scottish highlands, which her name suggested - but on the milder south-western seaboard. There a sailor ancestor had once been blown aground and, having escaped the attentions of the wreckers whose machinations had brought his vessel to grief, had decided to settle down amongst them rather than face up to the further risks of a life afloat again.

Shunning the farming life her parents had brought her up to, Sarah yearned for big city life; leaving home at eighteen to realise that ambition. Her build and her moral values had guided her towards a career in law enforcement, a role she had settled into as naturally as if she had always belonged. WPC Mackenzie was patrolling Middleton Hall grounds on foot.

4

Phil Thomsett was also a member of the local constabulary and, like Sarah, was patrolling the grounds of the Hall. Unlike her, however, he was doing his patrolling in comfort - behind the wheel of a slow moving squad car.

Phil had been the twelfth, and so far the latest, member of the local force to proposition Sarah. Still entertaining the hope that she might yet change her mind and succumb to his advances, he was studying her speculatively as he drove up behind her. She certainly had strong thighs and an attractive bottom. He had once stroked one of those thighs for a few brief, glorious moments of promise, before Sarah had firmly pushed his hand away. He was reliving the moment in his mind when, without any warning, a hooded figure emerged from the rhododendrons to the left of the park, casually exposed himself to WPC Mackenzie, and then plunged back into the undergrowth to the right of the path with the policewoman in hot pursuit.

It was all so unexpected and unbelievable that PC Thomsett had driven on a hundred yards or so before the facts registered. He jerked the car clumsily into reverse, careering wildly back along the path, but by the time he had reached the point where it had all happened, there was no sign of either of them. After a moment of indecision the young policeman returned sadly to his car and radioed in to the police station for reinforcements.

Sarah, meanwhile, was homing in on her prey. Her utter astonishment at being the target of a flasher had been total, but it had lasted a split second - no more. Then she had plunged into the woods, hard on the heels of the hooded figure whose apprehension was her destiny.

5

George Riodan was the third of the Middleton Hall park attendants. A pale, slight Irishman, he had brought being off sick to a fine art; having attended on only forty-eight days out of a possible three hundred and ten during the previous year.

George suffered from nervous debility. A nebulous complaint, which involved many tearful confessions to his doctor that he was unable to cope with the pressures of his life, and one or two well choreographed twitching collapses in front of him, before his performances were rewarded with the ultimate accolade of a sickness certificate whenever he wanted one. George's doctor was not a weak man but, as he confessed to his wife after one particularly trying session with his patient, it had come to the point of accepting George's performances at face value, or becoming a genuine victim of the complaint himself.

The council, as George's employers, had entertained doubts about the accuracy of his ill-health on several occasions; having once gone so far as to instruct him to attend their own doctor for a second opinion. George was actually on his way to see the man when he suffered such an acute attack of claustrophobia that he had to leave the bus he was on and make his way back home to recover. Travelling by public transport was out of the question after that, of course, and, since the doctor was based too far away for George to make his way there by bicycle, the council was obliged to drop the whole sordid business. George was left alone to make his occasional appearances at work, pick out a broom from one of the many he had stashed in various hiding places around the grounds, and commence sweeping paths from the point where he had left off two or three months earlier.

It was typical of WPC Sarah's luck that the day she seemed about to achieve her destiny ahead of schedule by apprehending the hooded figure, now no more than a yard ahead of her and visibly slowing, was the same day that George had decided his condition had improved enough to warrant a return to work.

George had hidden his broom under a large shrub along the rhododendron walk when he had last been taken poorly. Ten weeks had passed since then and broom and branches had somehow contrived to become entangled. The slim Irishman was deep in the bush, giving a final heave to the handle of the broom, when the panting flasher puffed past unnoticed. There was a crack like a rifle shot and rhododendron, George and broom all parted company. The bush, having shaken off its assailant, to spring back upright as if nothing had ever happened. George, to tumble head over heels backwards until he came to rest in a heap of leaf mould. The broom, to fly like a missile, straight between the ankles of the policewoman reaching out an arm to grasp her quarry.

Sarah was not amused. She made that very clear to George. By the time the attendant had finished being on the receiving end of a tongue lashing from the disappointed officer his condition had deteriorated so badly he was unable even to hide his broom before making his unsteady way to the attendants office to sign off and return home.

6

Dave Croftman wasn't very happy either. Not when he returned to the park after his latest midday excursion and discovered the grounds overflowing with the local police force. He was especially unhappy when a particularly officious sergeant asked him what he had in the bag he was carrying, then checked to see if Dave was telling the truth.

Before the end of the afternoon the park, already abuzz with various accounts of the latest appearance of the hooded flasher, was buzzing still further with the additional excitement of the arrest of Croftman, apparently responsible for the spate of house breaking in the area.

Simon, who had thought his life to be as bleak as it was possible to be, plunged to still greater depths of despair when he heard the news. Pensively wondering what John Death would make of this further evidence of the indiscipline he considered rife in Simon's area.

CHAPTER NINE

Mr Death, as it happened, was having troubles of his own. So much so that he only gave the business of Croftman's arrest the most cursory of glances in passing. Completely overlooking the capital that could have been made of it at Simon's expense. As if bad fortune, being contagious, was acting to strike down everyone connected with Middleton Hall, Mr Death was facing a crisis of his own.

Despite popular opinion in the park to the contrary, the maintenance manager was, at heart, someone who wished to be at peace with the world, accepted at face value and appreciated for all he did for his staff. Far from being the person someone had once unkindly described as, 'all window-dressing and bullshit', John Death was, in his own estimation, a man who cared. Totally unlike Gerald Wilson, who suffered headaches and plunged to deep depths of depression whenever he felt the pressures of work building, Death knew himself to be capable of taking punishment, as well as handing it out.

The unfortunate thing about the man was his complete inability to communicate these opinions and ideals to other people. Probably why he could never exist in unison with Simon Spaulding, with whom he was just too much of a kind. Each considered his ideas to be right and just. Each resented their being questioned by other people.

Simon, of course, considered Death to have the upper hand in forcing his ideas on the park by virtue of his senior position. John suspected Spaulding of adopting a position of non-compliance with management policy and deliberately hindering his (John's) ideas by misdirecting the efforts of the workforce.

"If only," Death often spoke to himself in his darker moments, "people would try to see and understand." So often they seemed to deliberately misunderstand his motives in changing inefficient systems of work, which had pootled along aimlessly for far too many years, or taking out features which had grown old and tired, and replacing them with streamlined schemes that were less of an affront to a forward planning parks manager.

One cross was heavier than any of the others Death bore in the course of his employment. It was the one forcing him to recognise that, of all his Middleton Hall workforce, only Joseph Grubb seemed to sense enough of the man behind the mask of parks manager, to proffer the hand of friendship to his chief. John did not like Joseph Grubb - or his fawning, fussing ways. He suspected they would have been on offer to whoever filled his shoes, whatever their beliefs. Not that he didn't prefer Grubb to the undisciplined and sullen Spaulding, but it was a marginal preference, and the manager tried not to encourage Maggot in any way.

Other people didn't always realise that of course. They saw Maggot hanging about John Death, waiting on his every word, then heard the former's account of what had passed between the two of them in private. Everyone could see that Maggot was more in demand with the manager than Simon, who should have been. Despite Death's belief that he remained completely fair and unbiased in his dealings with his staff, the picture painted by misinterpretation and hearsay indicated a state of affairs completely at odds with that.

Perhaps if Death had had the kind of wife with whom he could share his problems, then he might have learned the skill of communicating with other people. Gillian had not turned out to be the wife he'd been looking for in marrying her, however. There were times when John would ponder on what had become of her. The laughing girl who had pulled down his trousers with cries of, 'Death where is thy sting?' Was she really the same sarcastic, headache-ridden woman who shared his home? Somewhere along the years their marriage had seized up like a rusty hinge neither of them was bothered enough about to oil.

Gillian, for her part, had no great need of her husband. Only the measure of independence from her lover his existence gave her. Christian was a shaggy-headed Scandinavian she had picked up in a singles bar in the city one evening.

John was always too tired by work to trouble his wife sexually. His only threat to her being the boredom resulting from his obliging her to listen to endless accounts of his professional triumphs. (If he had failures he never mentioned them and Gillian didn't care enough to ask.) Christian was a moderately successful writer who could, and perhaps might, have supported her if she had ever chosen to leave her husband. Gillian, however, preferred not to tamper with the status quo. On those occasions when Christian's appetite proved a little too much for her to stomach she was glad of a bolthole from his excesses to which to run.

John Death, of course, knew nothing of his rival. He was aware his wife went out rather more than she used to. He knew she had a special friend he had never met, always referred to as C, which he took to be short for Carol or Christine, but in that his marriage varied in no way from those of most of his contemporaries. Content to allow things to drift with the prevailing currents, Death gave his mind over to more important matters. The possible repercussions of his recent site meeting with Warren Hescott for a start.

Councillor Hescott had never been a man to let the grass grow under his feet. When he saw trouble looming he sought to seize the initiative by charging it head on. Aware that the parks officer responsible for organising the celebration of his years in office seemed intent on promoting his opinion of what was a suitable tree to be planted, to the detriment of Hescott's own ideas, he determined on a sniping and skirmishing campaign to force Death to toe the line.

It didn't take Hescott's vociferous concern very long to drive Gerald Wilson to distraction. "John isn't getting the best out of the situation," he confided to Peter Gormann over coffee one Friday morning.

Gormann nodded understandingly, noting the number of tablets the other man was shaking into the palm of his hand from a small bottle he'd taken from an inside pocket.

It was Gormann's opinion Wilson was driving himself too hard and verging on a nervous breakdown by so doing. The blinding headaches were becoming more frequent. Only the day before Gormann had been sure he saw Wilson weeping over the capital estimates he was processing. Peter had no desire to see the other man crack up completely. The loss of his maintenance co-ordinator, apart from putting more work onto his own shoulders, could well provide an opening for John Death. Gormann didn't want that. Despite his professed spiritual beliefs, he could muster little Christian love for Death, who he much preferred not to be treading on his heels. He decided to support the ailing Wilson by manoeuvring the pressure onto the other man instead.

"I begin to wonder whether John's appointment wasn't a mistake all round." Gormann had a way of seeming to consider each word in turn before setting it free into the world. "Audit have been making their feelings felt about the amount of money being spent on nurseries since John joined us. There seems to have been a great imput of resources, without any additional output of plants."

"I know Peter, I know," the older man leaned forward earnestly, "but the chief seems to have given him carte blanche to do as he pleases in regard to nursery improvements."

"Mr Potter doesn't have to face Treasurers and try to explain away the results of that policy." The assistant director, made brave by the knowledge that his boss was away at a seminar in Blackpool, gave vent to his feelings. "John is going to have to be made aware that our purse has a bottom to it after all. Do you realise that last month he spent five hundred pounds on plant labels alone?"

"Preposterous." Wilson agreed, brightening perceptibly. "Especially if you notice how many of them are finding their way onto the compost heaps when plants are thrown out. How much trouble would it be for staff to remove the labels and use them again?"

"Ah, but can you really expect them to do that when they can see so much waste all around them? John must be made to cut back on purchases of that nature. It's the only way to make staff aware that finances are tight."

"He'll appeal to the chief." Wilson was suddenly gloomy again.

"Fortunately Mr Potter is too far away to hear him," Gormann risked a brittle smile, "and there is the business of Councillor Hescott's tree. Even John won't withstand the backlash if that's fouled up and Hescott reneges on his deal over Blacks Meadow."

"So you think..."

"I think we'd best get the ball into John's court whilst the director is safely out of the way. Then hope that something happens to upset his applecart before Mr Potter returns from Blackpool.

Tell John to arrange a site meeting with the councillor for tomorrow."

Memory of that site meeting still rankled in Death's mind even though it had taken place several days before. It hadn't been his fault that he had been late. Sometimes he wondered whether Gillian deliberately tried to make things bad for him by failing to set the alarm clock for the correct time, or mislaying the keys to his car after using it the previous evening. Trust Spaulding to have taken advantage of the situation, Death ruminated bitterly. Ingratiating himself with Hescott and filling the old fool's mind with malicious propaganda about him as likely as not. His thoughts about the Middleton Hall supervisor plunged on to deeper and darker depths.

Simon, whilst suspecting he was the subject of such brooding attention from his immediate superior, naturally considered himself innocent of any such crime.

The young man had not been over pleased to see Councillor Hescott bearing down on him that morning. Since the arrest of Dave Croftman he had been avoiding John Death. Having to stay with the councillor until his manager arrived would make any further evasion impossible. Forcing a meeting between them he would rather not have had.

"Simon, isn't it?" Hescott had long ago learned the value of remembering faces and being able to put names to them with ease. He smiled warmly as he greeted the younger man. "Death not here yet?"

"He phoned a few minutes ago to say he'd be late. He's held up in traffic somewhere I believe. He lives a long way out in the sticks and has quite a drive into work every day."

Snort from Hescott. "Serve him right then. Should always live on your own patch, I say. I could never understand politicians who only go to see their constituents when an election is in the offing. Council officers are pretty much the same. If you've pride in a place you'll want to do your best for it and when you've done that you'll want to live there so you can share in the benefits.

Still, I mustn't bore you with an old man's ideas and foibles. I've no doubt we've both got plenty of other things to do. We'll just have to get on without the help of your governor. That all right with you?"

"He did ask if we could wait for him." Simon answered unhappily.

"And I say we can't." Hescott frowned. "I've a busy day today and my time is precious. I only managed to fit this meeting in at all because I've had to take up jogging on health grounds. Twice around the lake every morning since last Friday. What do you think of that?"

Simon, who had wondered about the tracksuit hanging loosely on his companion's bony frame, muttered something unintelligible by way of response, which the latter obviously took to be a compliment, because he smiled and then went on. "This morning I've stopped between circuits to discuss where this tree of mine is going to be sited. And discuss it I intend to do. Whether with you, or with Mr Death, is immaterial. Now what ideas have you got about where to plant the thing?"

Simon shrugged. "I thought somewhere on the back lawn," he admitted.

"Then let's take a look at it. Lead on."

It was some forty minutes later that John Death came hurrying across the lawn from the direction of the nursery, looking unusually hot and dishevelled after his hurried journey. "I'm sorry about this," he began his apology the instant he was within earshot of Hescott and Simon, who were standing looking down the slope of the lawn towards the lake. "I hope I haven't inconvenienced you too much by being so late."

"I'm happy to say you haven't inconvenienced me in the slightest, Mr Death," The councillor turned a triumphant eye on the new arrival. "I've enjoyed an interesting chat with Simon and we've agreed that the choice position for my tree would be just to the right of the main building, where its corner juts out into the lawn over there. It won't interfere with the maintenance of the grass at all, and will be in keeping with the more mature cedars across the way.

Isn't that so Simon?"

The latter nodded dumbly and tried not to catch his manager's eye. "But I thought...." Death began, shooting looks of intense annoyance at his supervisor. His protest was cut short. Hescott swept on unheedingly.

"So we've done our part Mr Death - but what about you? Have you come to an agreement with Gordon yet?"

"No, not yet councillor," Death admitted warily. "But negotiations are proceeding." He made a rather heavy-handed attempt at humour.

"Stuff and nonsense! If I know anything at all about you, they haven't even begun. I told you once before that I'm too old a bird to be taken in by the flannel that seems to be your stock in trade. I suggest you try it out on old Gordon and see if you have more success with him. I hope you do for your sake. It's only a week or two to the circus now and it won't look so good for you if we have to hold it without that tree.

Now, I've wasted enough time over this business for one morning, so I'll bid you good day. Nice seeing you again Simon." Pressing home Death's total lack of favour, he jogged off slowly and unevenly across the lawn towards the bridge.

"I gave him your message," Simon correctly interpreted the look on his chief's face and defended himself before any accusations could be made.

Death turned on his heel and stalked back towards the nursery yard without a word. Uncertain what his next move in the affair should be, he entertained no hope at all of wheedling the tree out of Mr Gordon. The latter had suffered as much at Death's hands as anyone. Dislodged from the various sheds and garages he had once occupied in the nursery area, deprived of a rusted but cherished Ford of ancient vintage, a collection of wine bottles (empty) built up over thirty years, and the bedstead on which he and his wife had consummated their marriage, he would obviously delight in withholding something so dearly desired by the perpetrator of those crimes.

Mr Death didn't dare even approach him with a request for assistance. What he had done was to commission Maggot to steal the tree on his behalf. It was a desperate measure to adopt, but the man was only too well aware that failure to procure the Cedar, by whatever means, would swiftly lead him to desperate times.

Maggot, of course, whilst accepting the commission had never intended to carry it out himself. Instead he subcontracted to Dave Croftman, who had still been in the planning stage when circumstances had robbed Maggot of his expertise. Faced now with the prospect of carrying the venture on his own shoulders, Maggot was beginning to wish he had taken more interest in Croftman's side of things, not spent his time planning the changes he would make to the park once he had ingratiated himself into Simon's job.

Death, meanwhile, having compounded the felony by the issue of his warrant, had been conducting interviews for a successor to Maggot's erstwhile accomplice and was complacently satisfied with his new park attendant. It had been the first time the manager had encountered such a pleasant spoken and intelligent person when interviewing for a lower manual position. Simon, in his place, would probably have said, 'horses for courses,' and made a more natural selection, but John Death, intent on improving the image of his workforce, was happy with his choice.

Len Saunders was far from happy when he found the new employee awaiting him in the nursery yard on the following Friday morning - the council's week began on a Friday, because this in some way suited the computer lurking in the bowels of the Civic Centre.

"Good morning Mr Saunders," Arnold Lovett's smile threatened to split his face in two.

"Op it," Len made a threatening gesture with his fist. "I haven't the time to bother with you this early in the morning."

"But I work here now. I'm your new park attendant."

"There's nothing I can do about it Len," Simon explained when the angry senior attendant stormed into his office a few minutes later. "I can't hire or fire anyone anymore. I'm not even invited to the interviews. You'll have to take the matter up with Mr Death."

"A lot of bloody good that will do. He probably took the bastard on to spite me in the first place. Sod it! You know what will happen as soon as my back's turned. Holes everywhere! And what about my days off? He'll be able to do as he pleases."

"I know Len," Simon said pacifically, "I'll try to have an eye kept on him but..."

"It'll finish me - the worry of that man. You see if it doesn't!"

Arnold Lovett bided his time and was a model attendant from the first. In vain Simon and Len pleaded with John Death, who was not a man to be swayed from a decision made. Arnold looked on and laughed in the knowledge that time *was* on his side and his chance must come. He rechecked his calculations and measured them out pace by pace whilst on his daily patrol. His spade was hidden in a convenient shrub nearby. No one could have been more prepared for anything. Arnold did not intend to be found wanting when opportunity finally knocked.

Maggot, meanwhile, also awaited a chance, which must surely come.

CHAPTER TEN

Carol Elizabeth Trennick hummed quietly to herself as she went about her business in the tumbledown greenhouses which, despite John Death's over-exuberant use of departmental capital for nursery improvements, still made up the bulk of the Middleton Hall nursery complex.

Carol Elizabeth was marvelling just how much difference a few short weeks had made to a life stretching out so mundane and unglamorous before her Tom had swept her off her feet. Carol was almost certain she was in love with him. Lack of previous experience being all that made her unsure. The slight degree of doubt remaining was negligible in any case. Not enough to spoil her mood, or to prevent her humming as she passed through the day reliving the special moments she had shared with her man the previous evening.

Tom, once he had negotiated the bashful first moments of their relationship, had proved to be an inventive lover. Too inventive for Carol's total peace of mind; he coupled his typical Sagittarian directness with a lively imagination, which didn't always require council issue protective clothing to stimulate it. By and large though, Carol's memories were pleasant ones, and she often smiled over them as she survived the days impatient for the evenings. For the first time in her experience she was content with her life and greeted each new day with expectation instead of the bored disinterest of former times.

Across the yard at the entrance to the men's mess room, Henry, Peter and one or two other men were arguing boisterously. Carol glanced across at them, experiencing the unaccustomed feeling that what they were discussing was in some way connected with her. It was another new experience for Carol to feel self-conscious around her male colleagues. One she didn't enjoy. She was about to turn away from them, to cover her embarrassment, when she noticed Henry detach himself from the rest of the group and stroll casually across towards her. Holding a paper at arm's length in front of him, he studied it, glanced at her, and then looked back at the paper again several times.

"Any idea of the time Carol?" There was something blatantly offensive about Henry's manner, though his words were innocuous enough.

"Twenty past ten," Carol glanced pointedly across the other's shoulder, towards the electric clock on the wall above the entrance to the men's mess room.

"Thanks." With a final steady appraisal, which sent the colour flushing to her cheeks with its unwanted intimacy, Henry nodded and made his way back to the knot of men gathered outside their mess room. Larking and sparring with each other like schoolboys on an outing, their unaccountable attitude left Carol feeling prickly and irritable, her carefree mood sullied and spoiled.

"Well?" Peter demanded of Henry as soon as he reached them.

"I'm sure of it." The others laughed and resumed their huddle around him.

"No work to do?" Simon Spaulding joined the group and was promptly inaugurated into whatever it was that was so interesting. Carol strained her ears for a clue to their preoccupation. "Where did you get it?" She heard Simon ask.

"Maggot found it in a waste bin," Peter replied with a quick glance towards Carol, who made a pretence of being totally immersed in her work.

Hilarity continued amongst the men for a few minutes more before Simon dispersed them. Covert glances raked the cold frames where Carol bent about her business as they went. Only Henry remained behind to pause beside the staff notice board for a moment. Hurrying off in the wake of the others once his business was complete.

Silence returned to the nursery yard. Carol recommenced humming as she returned to her private thoughts. Melody appeared from the direction of the conservatory and glanced at the notice board in passing, checked and returned to look again. She turned towards Carol, hesitated, shrugged and continued on her way across towards the nursery garden without a word.

Carol paused in her work and wiped her hands on a cloth she kept in her back pocket for the purpose. Her interest was aroused and she wanted to know what it was that everyone seemed to associate with her.

The page from a magazine, which Henry had pinned up on the notice board, bore the heading *'Readers Wives'* in bold type. It featured a number of photographs of women of varied ages and appearance, each openly displaying their sexual organs to the lens with a frankness that did them no credit. In the centre of the page, circled by a ring of red and green stars, Carol saw herself wearing nothing but her wellington boots and a smile. The rubber respirator standing between her buoyant breasts added a bizarre quality to the photograph, which had won the special award for that week. In the background, the tumbled Temple of Modern Virtue stood, predictably, in ruins.

Carol remembered that photograph. It was one of several Tom had taken of her with his little Polaroid. The one he had always declared to be the best. He hadn't told her he was so pleased with it he intended sharing its delights with the world. With a trembling hand she tore down the banner of her naivety and retired with it to the ladies rest room. There she reduced the offending item to tiny pieces, flushing them down the toilet before collapsing on the sofa in despair.

For the first time since meeting Tom, Carol didn't venture out into the park that dinnertime. Though resolving, amidst her tears, that she would have this thing out with her lover at the earliest opportunity, when it came to the point the old Carol won the day. Unable to face Tom, or any of the other men she would have to pass in order to get to him, she remained in the women's rest room. At least there she would only have to face Melody. Someone who, sharing the same physical attributes as herself, could be relied on to show less interest in them than the men did.

As it turned out she lunched alone, planning the sickness which would get her out of the public eye. Melody had fully intended to be there to pick up the pieces of her workmate's emotions but had been coerced into going out with Simon Spaulding instead.

2

Simon hadn't intended to invite Melody to repeat their previous dinnertime fiasco and was as surprised as she was when he heard the words come out. The simple fact of the matter, which the man recognised, however hard he then tried to ignore it, was that he was missing Christine more than he had thought was possible. Melody was no more than a substitute in a situation where no substitute was possible. It had been irresponsible and unfair of him to embroil her in his emotional problems and reject her out of hand in the same easy movement, but that was what he had done. He didn't want to talk to her. He didn't want to talk to anyone. He wanted to be alone and yet he had saddled himself with a companion.

Melody, on the other hand, had welcomed the invitation at first, seeing in it a second opportunity to throw herself on her supervisor's mercy by putting her case to him. It hadn't turned out that way. Her opening attempts at a conversation that could be guided towards broaching the unbroachable were rejected with such finality she found herself wondering why, if Simon felt so unsympathetic towards her, he had sought to torture her with his company in the first place.

"Find someone else." Had been Christine's final words to Simon when they had spoken briefly on the telephone the previous evening. "I'll only hurt you if you don't. Barry's my husband and my life has to be with him now, so stop trying to hang on to what we had. It's over Simon. Please try to see that and let go. You'll soon find someone more suited to you, I promise you. Goodbye my love." Christine was an avid reader of romantic fiction and was unconsciously modelling herself on a heroine who had given up her true love in favour of an arranged marriage, which helped to save an empire.

All of which was of little consolation to Simon - even if he had known the real reason for her behaviour. Christine had told him to forget her once before. On that occasion he had refused to consider marrying her because, as he quite reasonably pointed out, she was already married to Barry. Christine had slated him for only wanting her for sexual gratification and it had taken Simon a long time to talk her into giving him another chance. Now he faced a second major crisis in their relationship and, whilst assessing the battered state of that emotional vehicle, had come face to face with the possibility that he was growing tired of the constant battle against Christine's moods and fancies. Her insistence on putting her family's interests before his had always jarred on the man, but now he found the resentment it aroused in him difficult to control.

Simon was fond of Christine and prepared to give way in preference to her sons, but he baulked at extending the same privilege to her husband. It was an impossible situation and he was reflecting on its possible outcome when Melody broke in on his train of thought.

"Simon." She said with sudden decision.

"What?" He answered sharply, impatient at being drawn away from choices that had to be made.

The small spark of courage, which had spurred Melody to come out in the open and make a clean breast of her problem, died. Extinguished by her companion's tone. "It doesn't matter," she answered dejectedly. "No really!" When Simon, stung to compunction by her total collapse, rephrased his rejoinder more invitingly. "It was nothing."

3

Maggot observed their return with interest and filed away for future reference this knowledge of a second dinner spent together. He intended to keep it to himself for the time being and not repeat the mistake of reporting it in the mess room. Let the other men's ignorance of what was going on continue until he found it useful to disclose the facts. Maggot considered that he had enjoyed a profitable dinner hour. A seedy little man, hanging about the area of the temple, had just accosted him and asked after Carol.

Maggot, already interested in Tom, was even more interested by the camera hanging about his shoulders. It looked quite capable of having taken the photograph of Carol, which had excited so much interest when found. The likelihood of a connection between them was strong and Maggot hoped it might prove another aid to discipline when he was eventually appointed supervisor. That moment was almost within reach now. The old reprobate could feel it in his water.

He had even managed to put together an alternative plan for gaining possession of Councillor Hescott's tree, now that Dave Croftman had been removed from the running.

It had always been Mr Gordon's practice, when he and his wife went on holiday, to invite Maggot to stay at his house in the role of caretaker, to prevent any possibility of burglary during their absence. The Gordons were as avid and all-encompassing collectors of everything and anything as a pair of magpies, and there were several items of real value amongst the dross with which they had surrounded themselves over the years.

The holiday this year was to take the form of a late summer tour of northern France in the battered Land Rover that had carried the couple all over the world during the past twenty years. Never for a moment suspecting that the man whom he had rescued from acute alcoholism now served a new master equally well, Mr Gordon intended to extend his customary invitation to Maggot to take possession of his home. The old man looked on his annual gesture as distributing largesse. Maggot, he knew, would have no other opportunity to be surrounded by so many interesting things. His supposed beneficiary, on the other hand, saw it as being put upon by a former employer, still unable to give up his role as Lord of the Manor. He resented the attitude and welcomed a chance to get even with his unsuspecting benefactor.

In the satisfaction and certainty of success, Maggot chalked up every slight and score he would need to settle when he reached his goal, pouring over them like a miser with his gold as he awaited the annual summons with uncharacteristic enthusiasm.

4

Arnold Lovett was finding it difficult to retain *his* enthusiasm in the face of the plethora of dirty jobs to which Len Saunders was subjecting him. Both men were fully aware that there must come a time when Arnold would be alone, with the park at his mercy. Both were equally aware that there was little chance Len could break Arnold's spirit before that moment arose. The senior attendant was a sportsman, however, prepared to rise to the challenge.

As he scraped the caked excreta from toilet walls, Arnold desperately struggled to retain the image of a golden cockerel in his mind. As he argued with bye-law-breaking visitors, or delved deep into litter bins filled to their brims with unsavoury items, Arnold kept reminding himself of the waiting fame. It would be his! He would succeed! With all he was suffering in his quest to own the idol, Arnold couldn't conceive of fate being so unjust as to allow him to fail.

CHAPTER ELEVEN

The weekend of the second sale of surplus plants from Middleton Hall nursery fell just a week or so after Carol's retirement from life's stage. It was an event John Death had decreed was to be even more successful than the first had been.

There had never been enough plants truly surplus to requirements to service the initial sale. Stock intended for planting in the parks and open spaces had been robbed to cover its needs. In order to provide the public with a wider choice on this occasion, Death had issued instructions for suitable specimens to be lifted from their positions in the beds and borders of the district parks, and containerised for sale. The manager of the south district was intent on making a gigantic splash successful enough to mitigate the machinations of Gormann and Wilson, who he believed to be out for his blood.

Simon watched the removal of plants from the Hall borders with a cynical detachment far removed from the anger earlier alterations had stirred up in him. He was surprised to discover that he really didn't care. It didn't matter to him in the slightest what happened to his cherished gardens now. The various aspects of his life had conspired to rob him of his spirit and John Death, had he but known it, was close to defeating Simon then. An all-out attack could have eliminated the supervisor from his consideration for all time, leaving the way open to install a more supportive replacement in the key Middleton Hall position.

Death was too involved in organising his extravaganza to give any thought to Simon, however. So total had the latter's opposition been to all of Death's schemes that he hadn't even considered allowing Simon the opportunity to take part in either preparation or sale. Instead he was drafting in staff from all over the south district to paint, mend, or move anything that might offend the public eye by its condition.

It was a pity about the car park, which had risen like a phoenix from the ashes of his redevelopment, he thought to himself, as he stood in the middle of it, watching his nursery staff hurrying and scurrying past him like ants with the top of their hill removed.

The nursery yard had been completely redesigned. The gnarled box trees, which had given it much of its character, grubbed out and burnt. The ancient mulberry tree, which Joseph Paxton, himself, was said to have planted, bulldozed down and removed. The vast car park the resultant empty space had made a viable proposition of was certainly impressive, but of little utilitarian value. A bye-law, forbidding the intrusion of private vehicles into the grounds, prevented use of the car park by anyone other than the drivers of staff cars and lorries. And they had fitted quite adequately into the former, more discreet, parking area.

At least the nursery itself had been improved by the removal of rows of elderly fruit trees dating back to the days of the nineteenth century kitchen garden, Death reflected sagely. The polythene tunnels were of much more use than a few otherwise extinct varieties of apples and pears. When he had found a way to prevent the geraniums grown in them from going leggy and developing stem rot, there would be much less wastage of plants for Gerald Wilson to be constantly harping on about.

Still, not everything in his life was so bleak. John Death shrugged off his dark humour as he remembered that Joseph Grubb had hinted that the Cedar from Gordon's garden was as good as safely in his hands and Gillian had been more responsive to his overtures this past day or two. She seemed to have quarrelled with her friend 'C' about something and hadn't been out in the evening since. He must remember to have a word with Gillian about those bruises on her wrists though. He'd noticed them when the sleeves of her cardigan had ridden up her arms as she was reaching for a pan from a shelf in the kitchen. They were unusual bruises, almost like rope burns to look at. She'd have to take care of them, or they might turn septic.

2

Melody assisted in the greenhouses for the first day of the sale. She had given up any hope of help from Simon and was facing the bleak prospect of pulling up her roots and starting a new life for the second time.

"Penny for them Melody."

The latter awoke to the world with a start, to discover Len Saunders standing in front of her smiling. She managed to force a smile in return, but her heart wasn't really in it.

"You looked a million miles away. Where were you? Back home?"

"Yes, I suppose I was." Melody's smile grew warmer at the thought of it.

"You should go back sometimes. I remember how it was when I first left home. It's hard to settle to new faces and new ways without any familiar ones to offset the change. You need the familiar things to put the unfamiliar ones in perspective sometimes. Besides, I expect they'd like to see you. How long is it since you last saw your mum?"

"I can't go back." Len Saunders was the only person Melody had encountered since moving south who had been genuinely friendly towards her for friendship's sake. She liked him and yet... How would he accept the revelation of the real reason she had left Bledstock?

Len shrugged. "I didn't mean to pry."

"I know that Len." Melody was angry with herself for the sharpness of her answer. "It was a nice thought, but going back now would only create more problems, not solve those I already have."

God, she thought to herself despairingly, as Len smiled understandingly and went off to check on Arnold Lovett. Why didn't I think of that little piece of philosophy before I wrote the damned letter?

Melody had committed an indiscretion she was afraid would lead to serious repercussions in her life.

Floundering in the depths of a truly overpowering attack of homesickness, she had written a letter to her mother. In it she had outlined most of what had happened to her since leaving Bledstock, including her present address, in case her mother should want to write to her in reply.

It hadn't been until the thick envelope was falling to the bottom of the pillar-box with a soft plop that the cold fear of foreknowledge had clutched at her heart. Only then did she remember how impulsive her mother could be and feel uncomfortably certain that the lady would never be content just to send a letter by return. Her mother would want to see at first hand the kind of a life that Gary was making for himself. (One of the details of her new life Melody had omitted to pass on, was the new identity she had adopted for herself.) To do that she would have to pay a visit to Middleton and Melody was not sure that she was ready to cope with such an emotional encounter yet.

The fear of what action her mother might take had weighed heavily on the girl for several days now, bringing down on her the previously unknown problems of insomnia and loss of appetite. When the flu germs struck, Melody had no resistance to offer. They were only one day into the plant sale when she was forced to cry off for the remainder of the weekend. Retiring to her bed in an attempt to sweat the illness out of her system.

The unfortunate girl wasn't missed as much as she might have been if Carol had managed to make her own sickness last as long as she had hoped it would. Carol was unfortunate in having a doctor of the old school, who believed in taking time to examine each patient properly whenever they visited him. It was a characteristic of his many of his patients found reassuring, but Carol was not amongst their number. Dr Witherstone had known her since she was a girl and, indeed, still seemed to regard her as one. He coughed and wheezed his way through a thorough examination before declaring her to be as fit as a flea and quite able to return to work.

There was little alternative for Carol but to comply. Her seven days self-certificated sickness had passed and to stay away any longer without the sanction of her doctor would lead to loss of pay and possible disciplinary action. She had made a reluctant return to the nursery and braved the initial smiles and sniggers, which had greeted her there. Interest in her anatomy, however, had swiftly died down to its previous level and things had settled back to the norm of her pre-Tom days. She hadn't seen anything of him since her return to work, having gone out of her way to avoid any route to or from work that might have risked an encounter with him. The sale had put a different complexion on the situation, however, and she was nursing the fear that Tom might visit it to purchase something and thereby force a meeting. She didn't think that she could bear anything of that nature in front of so many other people. As she bustled about, wrapping plants and taking money, Carol was keeping a wary eye open for her erstwhile lover, intending to make a strategic withdrawal if he appeared.

"Excuse me."

"Yes?" Wrapped up in her thoughts of Tom, Carol turned at bay, expecting to see him standing behind her. Instead, she looked down into the face of a small, elderly woman, who had tweaked her elbow in order to attract her attention.

"I'm looking for my son, Gary," the woman smiled expectantly.

Carol frowned. She considered she had enough worries to trouble her already, without the addition of eccentric customers making nuisances of themselves. "Should I know him?" She answered shortly, taking the plant a child with a runny nose was thrusting at her, checking it over and punching up the price on the till.

"He works here." The old lady replied with complete certainty.

The child had hurried off, clutching its purchase, and there was a temporary lull in business, so Carol had more attention to give to her inquisitor. "Gary?" She shook her head. "No one of that name works here. Are you sure that you have the right place?"

The smile slipped from her companion's face. "But he *does* work here," the woman protested, pink and indignant. "He wrote and told me so. He even mentioned about the sale. That was why I came here instead of going straight to his flat. Are you sure you're not mistaken? Gary his name is. Gary Carnforth."

Carol studied the other's face suspiciously for signs of a practical joke of some sort to follow up the business of her picture in the magazine, but it seemed innocuous enough. "We have a *girl* here named *Melody* Carnforth," she answered, taking care to display no emotion in case this *was* a trick. "But she isn't in today. She phoned in sick an hour or two ago."

The elderly woman stared at her open mouthed with dismay, as her face passed through every hue from existing pink to a deep brick red. "Oh Gary!" She ignored the man who pushed rudely past her to drop a brace of containerised Camellia plants onto the counter with a clatter. "What have I done? Why didn't you tell me?" Her voice died to an inaudible whisper, to which her lips still moved in accompaniment.

Carol, serving the man with his camellias, watched the woman with such morbid interest she overcharged for the plants and was obliged to refund the difference with an apology. "Are you all right?" She enquired solicitously, as soon as the two of them were alone again.

Mrs Carnforth awoke to the world with a start. "Oh my dear," she rested a trembling hand on Carol's arm. "It seems I have to throw myself on your mercy. What I've let slip to you - could you give me your solemn promise it will never go any further? Gary isn't a bad boy. He's never done any wrong by anyone in his life, but now I've done a great wrong to him in my innocence. Don't give Gary any reason to reproach me. Keep what I let slip to you a secret please!" She raised imploring eyes to the younger woman.

Carol considered the strange request carefully for several minutes before it finally dawned on her just what the other woman was getting at. A slow smile spread across her face. Here was something to divert minds from that photograph. Not that it seemed so important all of a sudden. At least by its display she'd been proved to be all woman. Little Melody was obviously something else again.

Mrs Carnforth seemed to follow the train of thought along its torturous route through Carol's mind. "It was too much to ask," she agreed sadly, as she turned and made her way back towards the exit, a picture of despair.

Stung to compunction by the total defeat in the other's mien, Carol made to go after her and deliver the requested promise, but was suddenly surrounded by a plethora of Chinese tourists clutching at her and demanding all manner of information about the plants on sale. By the time Carol had broken free from them, Mrs Carnforth was nowhere to be seen.

"What was that all about?" Maggot, who had arrived to relieve Carol for lunch just in time to catch the closing moments of Melody's mother's plea, sidled interestedly up to his workmate.

"What was all what about?" The latter, still undecided whether or not to honour the woman's wishes, feigned ignorance whilst she collected her thoughts and came to a decision.

"The old biddy who just ran out on you." The eternally questing finger probed the depths of Maggot's left nostril and Carol looked away. "Friend of yours was she?"

"Never saw her before," Carol spoke over her shoulder. "She was looking for her son Gary *Carnforth.*" She laid heavy emphasis on the second name.

"Oh." Maggot examined the end of his finger thoughtfully before inserting it into his other nostril. "Relative of Melody's do you think?"

"I think he *is* Melody." Making her mind up at last, Carol proceeded to divulge all that the unfortunate Mrs Carnforth had let slip.

Maggot smiled evilly as each i was dotted and every t crossed for him. "Something will have to be done about this." He fluffed himself up importantly.

"She hasn't actually done anyone any harm by it, you know." Carol suffered a sudden pang of conscience. "She probably can't help being the way she is."

"*He's* a sexual deviate. We can't let him just go on as if it doesn't matter." Maggot was enjoying himself now. "We have the safety of the public to consider. Mothers and children and..."

"Dogs?" Interrupted Carol unkindly, firmly regretting the alacrity with which she had passed on Melody's secret to Maggot. "Do you really think she's suddenly such a danger to everyone? She's just someone trapped in the wrong sort of body. It's sad, but there's nothing criminal about it."

"Isn't there?" Maggot asked portentously. "There would be if I had any say in the matter. And what about Spalding? Where does he come into all this? The two of them have been getting very chummy lately, spending their dinners together. Do you suppose he knows about all this? What sort of supervisor is that to have?"

"He might not have known," Carol defended Simon, but very weakly. "They could just be friends."

"Men don't spend their dinner hours with women - or even other men dressed up as women - simply out of friendship." Maggot assured her. And Carol was unable to find it in her heart to quarrel with his reasoning. "No, if this Carnforth person *is* a deviate, then Spaulding must be as well. Either way, Mr Death should be made aware of what's going on, so he can deal with it."

"Well I'm not telling him." Carol shrank from the pointed fingers which would follow the disclosure.

"That's okay." Maggot had never intended that anyone other than himself should enjoy the moment of revelation. "I'll see him for you. I don't want to any more than you do, but someone has to do these things." He turned to the lengthening queue of customers awaiting the end of their conversation with such a joyful smile wreathing his face that all but a few choked back their complaints about the poor service and smiled on him in return.

Carol wandered disconsolately off to her sandwiches and a few pages of Jane Austin, feeling overwhelmingly guilty at what she had done.

3

At home, in her sick bed, Melody threw back the covers and opened her eyes with a start, wondering what it was had disturbed her from her sleep.

CHAPTER TWELVE

Her first morning back at work after illness. Melody froze in the act of signing her name on the attendance sheet; a tingling sensation passing the length of her spine.

"Morning Gary."

So she hadn't imagined the words that had turned her to stone. She stirred her reluctant fingers into trembling action. Her usually neat signature became a squiggle, but other than that she hoped she'd given no sign.

"Bye Gary," the same hateful voice followed her to the door.

At the entrance to the female rest room Melody hesitated momentarily, then pushed the door open and went in. She couldn't understand what was happening to her and how Henry (she was sure it had been him who had spoken) had found out her real name. Mrs Carnforth had been unable to face her son after her *faut pas* with Carol. Hating herself for her weakness, she had, nevertheless, scuttled back to Bledstock, hoping that affairs, if left to themselves, would eventually break in Gary's favour.

Carol looked up as Melody entered. She had been wondering how best to react to the latter's arrival. A curt order to return to the male mess room where she more properly belonged, or pretend a total ignorance of the affair? Conscience decided her on the second course. She was aware that the part she had played in passing on what had been revealed to her in ignorance had dictated what would happen to Melody now. Disapproval, therefore, was tempered by remorse.

"Good morning Carol."

"Good morning...Melody."

The hesitation before the use of her alias did not go unnoticed by Melody but here, at least for the moment, was sanctuary. She sank into the soft cushions of the sofa, unconsciously positioning herself as far from Carol as she could get, and closed her eyes. She had no more than ten minutes before work began. In that time she had to gather together the scattered fragments of her life there and try to rebuild them into a new pretence to get her through the remainder of the day.

In his office, Simon was sitting on the desk, watching out of the window as a pair of jays sparred in the nursery garden, totally unaware of the latest crisis about to break on his head. It was an ignorance he was not permitted to retain for long. His staff, being generally unsure how familiar with Melody's true gender he already was, made no move to familiarise him with recent events, but John Death was subject to no such qualms.

The parks maintenance manager, having been primed by Maggot, was certain in his own mind just how deeply Simon was involved. Expecting his interview with the supervisor to be brief and merciless, he had been totally unprepared for the unfeigned disbelief with which his denouement was greeted and for the spirited denial with which Simon replied to his terse summing up of the situation.

Simon had survived beyond that lowest ebb of his fortunes with which he had been faced a day or two earlier and was now slowly picking himself up off the floor. The realisation of what John Death was insinuating stung him to a swift verbal counter attack, which culminated in a brief but vicious argument. When the two men took an acrimonious leave of each other twenty minutes or so later, Death was under no illusion that Simon was innocent of all charges, whilst Simon was angry and resentful that they had ever been laid.

To Melody, John Death showed a more merciful side of his nature. Partly through embarrassment at the whole sordid affair, and partly because, despite everything, his disapprobation of her was much less than that which he felt for Simon.

Melody, for her part, remained defiant throughout. Refusing to betray her feelings by as much as the quiver of her lip, or the moisture in her eyes. When the sentence of a week's notice was delivered, she accepted it with apparent equanimity. Later, however, alone in the rest room, she gave herself over to tears. She had loved working at the Hall and had been really beginning to believe her newest life would be a lasting one, once the stumbling block of the medical had been overcome. Now, overnight, it seemed an agent of whom she was still ignorant had destroyed all that. She would have to start again somewhere – but where? And what if that life then ended up the same? Melody was beginning to wonder if there was ever going to be an end to her purgatory.

Len, alone amongst the men, found sympathy for Melody's dilemma. "Poor kid." Was his immediate response when acquainted with the exciting scandal concerning her.

"Poor kid!" Henry mimicked cruelly. *"He's* a wierdo. A deviate!"* Maggot's over use of the latter expression had made it into something of a catch phrase in the park.

"So are people who use sex shops I suppose." Len studied him thoughtfully.

"What's that supposed to mean?" Henry retreated a little under the steady gaze.

"Only that I saw you coming out of the one along the High Street last Thursday. What was it Henry? Child porn? Bondage? What's *your* deviation?"

"Sod off!" Henry reddened under the attack. "I only went in there out of curiosity. Wanted to see what the place was like inside, that was all. I told you all about it didn't I?" He appealed to his unresponsive workmates who, having no wish to draw Len's fire, sheepishly ignored him. "We all had a laugh about it that afternoon." Henry's sense of humour was too over-developed for him to be very popular with the other men. They were enjoying his discomfiture until Maggot came to his aid.

"At least Henry doesn't dress up and try to pass himself off as something he isn't. Makes me shiver - that sort of thing."

"Used to make you shiver in a different way though didn't she Joe?" Len was content to fight on as many fronts as necessary. "Isn't that what needles you about her?" He goaded. "Thought you'd bitten into a Turkish delight, then found it was a caramel?"

"You can say what you please mate," Maggot steadfastly retained his aplomb. "What interests me is what Spaulding is going to do now. The way he's been sniffing around it, he must have been in the know. It stands to reason. What I say is, that if they sack one, they ought to sack the pair of them. I ask you. Who wants a queer for a supervisor?"

Simon was finding his thoughts following the same unhappy track. Though totally innocent of the slander Maggot was perpetrating against him, he felt his position to be a very delicate one indeed. He and John Death had swapped some very deep lying home truths, which would have done better to remain hidden. Now that his initial anger had passed, he was wondering if it would be possible to undo the damage done between them. Concentrating his mind on finding a solution to the problem, he was far from happy when a tap on the door was followed by the appearance of Melody in his office.

"I - I'm sorry." It had cost Melody a great deal to make the effort to go to see Simon. Having picked up an inkling of what was being said about the two of them, however, and realising that their being seen together by Maggot was more her fault than Simon's, she had felt it necessary to make the gesture. "I suppose I should have told you but..."

"But you didn't." Impatient for her to be gone, Simon completed the faltering sentence. "Forget it. I should have known."

"How could you?" Melody managed a whimsical smile at that. "Is it so obvious now that you know?" The smile faded as she realised Simon was looking any way other than at her. "Was Mr Death very hard on you about it?"

"He would have been if I'd let him. Maggot seems to have woven him a very imaginative picture of us. I had to put him right on a few points. He's given you a week's notice I hear."

"Yes. It was only to be expected I suppose."

"I'm sorry." Simon glanced from a point somewhere above her head to one about centre desk.

"I doubt that."

The responsive smile, which lit Simon's face, died quickly. "No, perhaps I'm not," he agreed soberly.

"I don't blame you for not wanting me around under the circumstances. I don't suppose you want me here now. Before I go though, can you just put me out of my misery? How did everyone find out?"

"From Maggot apparently."

"Yes but how...."

A knock on the door interrupted her and Len looked in. "I'm sorry -I'll come back."

"No Len. I was just going." She turned and almost ran towards the door.

"Melody," Len took a gentle hold of her arm as she rushed past and the girl looked up at him questioningly. "If things get too much for you, you're welcome to use the attendant's office for your breaks and the like. I don't mind - and Lovett hadn't better."

"Thank you." She found herself having to bite her lip in order to whisper her reply. Steeled to face censure, as she was, the unexpected evidence of understanding was more than she could handle.

"Well why not?" Len answered the unspoken criticism on Simon's face once they were alone. "Do we all jump just because Maggot tells us to? Besides, I feel genuinely sorry for the kid. It must be bad enough to be in the wrong sort of body to fit your emotions. Why make things worse by kicking the shit out of her because of it? I wouldn't even do that to Lovett." He reflected for a moment. "Well perhaps to him, but not to anyone else," he amended.

Simon managed a rueful smile at the tirade. "I just feel I've been made to look such a prize mug Len. Well you must know what everyone's saying about me now."

Len nodded. "So I do, but get things into perspective. It isn't Melody saying them - and what they're saying about her is worse. All right," he conceded, catching the interruption in Simon's eyes. "She's guilty and you're innocent, but she's also completely incidental to the whole affair. What you're looking at is Maggot trying to oust you from a job he honestly believes should be his. Melody was the catalyst, you were the cause and Maggot played you both like an artist."

"Maggot." Simon sighed and there was a wealth of meaning in the way that he said it.

"Maggot," Len agreed. "And it's time something positive was done about that man."

"Such as?" Simon challenged him.

"Well," the senior attendant glanced back out of the door before moving closer to Simon. "There's something I've had in mind for a long time. Maggot's got habits of his own which don't bear too much examination, though they fit his name to a T. He eats things he finds in litter bins. I've seen him do it!" He insisted, as Simon smiled in disbelief. "More than once when he's been on duty with me. I've often played with the idea of hiding something really nasty in a bin, just by way of a scientific experiment, and watching to see if he picks it out. Supposing, though, we were to put something attractive in a litter bin instead?"

"Laxative chocolate?"

"I was thinking more in terms of a packet of sandwiches. You can put all sorts of things into sandwiches. Bad cheese, rancid butter...."

"I know where I can get my hands on some purgative medicine we could soak everything in," Simon suggested dreamily.

Len smiled grimly. "He's on with me tomorrow night."

"That gives us twenty four hours to collect up anything that's suitable. I'll come round to your lodge at 4:30 tomorrow. We'll pool our resources and see what sort of a tit bit we can create out of them."

"It'll have to be special to pay him back for everything he's got coming to him."

"It will be Len. I can feel it in my bones."

2

As the conspirators capered about their cauldron like the witches in *Macbeth,* a more genteel council of war was taking place in Interview Room A at the Civic Centre. Peter Gormann and Gerald Wilson were discussing what was to be done about John Death.

Potter, the Director, had not been happy, on returning from his week in Blackpool, to be informed by the Parks Maintenance Manager (South), that the Assistant Director (Parks) and the Parks Maintenance Co-ordinator had been conducting a vendetta against him during their chief's absence.

The Director of Leisure Services had wasted no time in putting his dissatisfaction before the culprits. "I no expect to find when I've been away a wee while that you two comedians are spending your time buggering about the way you've been."

"But..." Wilson got no further before being savagely put in his place.

"Did I ask you to speak little man? Have you no the manners to hear me out before you start blathering your innocence? Innocence!" He spat in his indignation and Gormann exercised great self-control in refraining from wiping the saliva from his cheek. "Are your parks in such a fine state you've no need to be bothering your heads about them? Well? Have you no got a tongue anymore? You found it well enough when it wasna wanted." He deliberately directed the majority of his venom at Wilson, who he knew from experience to be the weaker of the two.

"T-there are n-no p-problems w-with the p-parks." Wilson had only recently started to stutter when put under pressure, but already the disability was more pronounced.

"Now there's a brave fancy for a man to enjoy." Potter's mouth smiled but his eyes didn't join in. "And what about Copse Hill? King James' Field? Middleton Hall?" He fired a random burst of names at Wilson on the safe assumption that the latter's incompetence would allow most of them to strike home.

"What complaints are those?" Gormann understood the ways of his chief better than Wilson did and interrupted to take the battle to the enemy.

As he had expected, Potter immediately retreated in confusion. "I've no the time to go into all that the noo," he blustered a defence, "it's enough for me to say that there have been complaints and that I'm not happy about the way things have been run in my absence. I'm looking for improvements from the two of you - substantial ones - or the next time I go away I might just leave John Death in charge of things instead of you."

There was much more in the same vein before Potter was finished, but it was noticeable that, whilst Wilson wilted under the onslaught, Gormann remained totally unmoved. The secret of his immunity was easily explained

- the assistant director simply wasn't listening. His mind was running on ahead of the present unpleasantness and planning reprisals against John Death.

"It has to be something big, something even Potter can't ignore," he confided to Gerald Wilson when the two of them were eventually released from the director's presence.

Wilson was suffering one of his headaches. A blinding one, which seemed to be lifting the top of his skull, and he couldn't really find the energy to plan revenge. He admitted as much to Peter Gormann and the latter exploded angrily.

"Pull yourself together Gerald! Are you just going to allow Death to get away with what he's done to us?"

"You heard what Mr Potter said as well as I did Peter," the older man protested. "What choice do we have?"

"We fight him man! We keep niggling away at him until we turn up something even Potter won't be able to ignore."

"And if we fail?"

"With Death?" Gormann snorted. "The man is so nefarious that would be an impossibility.

Yes Doris?" A tall, stern-faced woman had appeared silently at his side.

"The leaving forms for Melody Carnforth. John Death should initial them, but he isn't here today. Can you oblige?" She flourished a sheaf of pale blue papers in his direction.

Gormann sighed. "I'm even having to do the man's work for him now. All right Doris," he held out a hand, "leave them with me."

"I really wanted them completed now," the woman remarked disapprovingly.

Gormann chose to ignore her. "Who is Melody Carnforth?" he asked his companion as they continued on their way across the office.

Wilson obliged with the scandal concerning Melody. "So who employed her?" Gormann was suddenly alert.

"John Death I suppose," the other replied. "Why? There surely isn't anything for us there?"

"Probably not, but we can't afford to let it pass without investigation. Doris coming up to us the way she did might just have been divine intervention. Find this Carnforth person's starters forms, and anything else we have on him, and bring them to interview room A. We'll go over them with a fine toothed comb and see what we come up with."

It was several hours later before Gormann spoke again. "Death filled in these forms - it's his writing. Don't you see Gerald?" He reacted exasperatedly to the look of blank incomprehension, which was his companion's only reply. "We're sacking him for falsifying these forms, but can we prove he did that? Did John Death actually ask him what sex he is, or did he simply assume wrongly?"

"It's dreadfully weak," Wilson observed doubtfully.

"It's all we have," the other retorted with spirit, "and handled properly it could be enough. It gives a case with which to fight the dismissal and, since Death hired *and* fired the fellow, any mud which flies on account of it will land firmly on him."

"But supposing he doesn't want to fight the dismissal Peter?" Wilson was determined not to see light at the end of the tunnel so easily. "Under the circumstances he might well prefer to cut and run."

"Be damned to what *he* wants!" Gormann's eyes flashed angrily. "If he doesn't want his sexual leanings paraded in front of the world he should keep a better secret.

We've a chance here to settle John Death once and for all, and we're not going to let it pass simply to placate the finer feelings of some inconsequential freak of nature.

What union is he in?"

Wilson supplied his senior officer with the information from the personnel file in front of him.

"Perfect," Gormann rubbed his hands together contentedly. "Phil Wreston is their area officer and he owes me a favour or two. He's going to advise Carnforth to fight and we're going to supply him with the information to do it.

My God Gerald, just think of the possibilities of the situation. Women's Lib, Gay Rights - Transvestites Anonymous it there is one. They'll all want to get a finger in the propaganda to push their causes. It'll make the national newspapers for certain and probably television as well.

Whatever the outcome, it will make the name of John Death smell like a cess pit, and we'll be in the clear because - do you know where we're going to be when this thing breaks?" Wilson shook his head bemusedly. "On leave. Both of us. We'll book it today. Cheer up Gerald! Think of the look on Death's face when he realises what's hit him."

3

A white faced Maggot sat hunched up on the edge of his bed two mornings later, totally unaware of what had hit *him*. The victim had taken the bait, which Simon and Len had laid out for him, and despite the night being a constant passage between bedroom and toilet, the violent upheaval inside him still showed no sign of abating.

The conspirators noted Maggot's absence with unholy joy and Melody was grateful for a less obviously antagonistic attitude towards her without Maggot present to orchestrate the masses.

Later in the day news of another event was to push thoughts of Melody even further into the background of park life. Someone had at last been arrested on suspicion of being the flasher the press had glorified as the Middleton Hall rapist. With a wail of anguish, Carol discovered that the man taken into custody was none other than her Tom.

CHAPTER THIRTEEN

WPC Sarah Mackenzie hummed happily to herself as she patrolled her beat through the grounds of Middleton Hall. The sun shone in a clear blue sky, birds sang in the trees and along the length of the herbaceous border bees bustled busily from flower to flower. The embellishments to an already perfect day. Even without them Sarah's life would have been complete. Yesterday - and the girl was still unable to keep her feet touching the ground when she thought of it -she had finally achieved the ambition, which had been her driving force since graduating from police college, all of seven (Or was it eight?) weeks before. Yesterday WPC Mackenzie had singlehandedly arrested a notorious criminal.

The arrest had tasted especially sweet to Sarah. Her single-minded pursuit of the man had become common knowledge at the station and egos ruffled by her disinterest in their owner's sexual blandishments had soon made a joke of her ambition. Calling Sarah a man hater was the least of the labels attached to the girl.

Her unexpected success had been the cause of much jubilation at the station. Especially amongst those officers who had suffered most at the hands of women's lib groups, local residents associations and various other bands of citizens, who saw the continuing threat of there being a rapist at large in the park, even if it wasn't true, as a reflection of the inefficiency of the local police. At an impromptu celebration, held at the 'Earl's Buttons,' Sarah, as guest of honour, allowed herself to be plied with drinks until she became quite giggly and silly. A draw was swiftly organised amongst the men present and, as holder of the winning ticket, Inspector Murrow was able to offer Sarah a lift home in his car and become the first officer from the local station to enjoy her body to the full.

Sarah hadn't minded. It had never been in her nature to be celibate and Colin Murrow was far from being the first. It had simply suited her to keep her colleagues at bay whilst capture of the infamous felon was her main concern. Now that he was safely behind bars she was free to do her own thing again and intended that to include many more sessions of the kind she had enjoyed with the inspector.

Musing whether careful playing of Murrow would provide a lever to possible promotion in the future, Sarah had just decided that it very likely could, and was wondering how best to push ahead with the project, when she became aware of a movement amongst the birch trees and rhododendrons lying back from the path to her left.

Sarah's dancing progress came to a sudden halt; her mind awaking to alarm bells ringing. A dreadfully familiar figure in tracksuit and garish hood had emerged from the bushes, stood deliberately and provocatively staring at her for a moment, then turned and plunged back into the undergrowth.

Precious seconds were lost whilst Sarah remained rooted to the spot in disbelief that lightening could strike her twice in such a way. Then she crashed into the bushes in pursuit, only to meet a low-growing branch travelling in the opposite direction. Momentarily blinded as it struck her across the eyes, Sarah pulled up short. By the time the tears caused by the blow had cleared enough to allow her to continue the chase, the hooded figure was nowhere to be seen.

It was a bitter moment for the girl to face up to. In mounting desperation she scoured the woods from end to end without success. Carbon copy, or original, neither hood nor tracksuit were in evidence in the grounds anymore. Reluctantly, Sarah radioed in to control to acquaint him with what had occurred.

Defeat never tasted more sour than it did to the frustrated police constable acknowledging orders to quarter the grounds again and await the reinforcements being dispatched to her aid. Going dispiritedly about the pointless exercise, the thought occurred to Sarah, that the shenanigans of the previous evening might prove to have been a little premature after all.

In the days that followed the police became gradually aware that they were being persecuted in a strange and subtle way. Inspector Murrow, angry at having the arrest of the elusive criminal dangled before him, only to be snatched away again a few hours later, noticed it first. Whilst the masked Will o' the wisp was appearing at every opportunity to police officers of either sex who ventured into the grounds of the Hall, he seemed to be leaving the general public carefully alone.

Murrow spent long hours puzzling over the problem. At his request the best police psychologists were put in the picture, but proved unable to come up with an explanation that might help. He considered consulting a medium, but baulked at the extravagance of such a gesture, deciding in the end to rely on tried and trusted policing to win through in time. In twos, or threes and sudden surges the police swept through the grounds, but always the hooded and track-suited pimpernel remained one step ahead.

2

John Death paid little heed to the antics of either police or flasher. His mind was taken up by matters of far greater importance. The day of the tree planting ceremony was drawing closer and still the tree on which that old idiot Hescott insisted seemed no nearer being his.

Maggot had failed his master. The doctored sandwiches Len and Simon had prepared for him seemed to have set off a chain reaction throughout his entire digestive system, which continued to enforce his absence from work.

Simon he dared not ask for help in view of the acrimony which existed between them and the fear -

probably justified - that the supervisor would not only delight in refusing to assist but might well drop a hint to Gordon of what was in the wind. The desperate times, which the parks maintenance manager had feared, had come upon him now, and the desperate measure he was obliged to adopt to withstand them, was for he himself to remove the tree from Hereward Gordon's garden.

He made his plans carefully. Mr Gordon, he discovered, attended classes at the local adult education centre every Thursday afternoon. Mrs Gordon, taking advantage of her husband's absence, always spent the day visiting friends. Basing his actions on this information, John Death got certain arrangements of his own under way.

He began by organising a refresher course for his nursery staff at Cromwell Heath, the other nursery boasted by his southern district. That would ensure that most of the eyes, which might otherwise be prying, would be occupied elsewhere when he went into action. Simon, he instructed to do an in depth examination of playground equipment at a site some miles away from Middleton. The remaining parks staff should have no reason to be in the nursery area anyway and Death intended to give short shrift to any that were.

It was a well-planned venture, but as Potter could have told him in the words of his national bard, they are the ones which so often 'gang agley.' There was one witness John Death had not allowed for. Mr Gordon had been obliged to put his vehicle into a garage in order that certain essential repairs beyond his capabilities could be carried out. The old man had decided that travelling to his class by any other means was quite out of the question and had spent the afternoon working in his garden instead.

John Death checked the nursery area carefully for stragglers before he made his move. Arnold Lovett found himself sent out into the park in search of cyclists, despite his legitimate protest that it was his dinner hour. Peter

Gilray was told to go and cut down the Japanese polygonum growing along the bank of the lake, despite his less acceptable excuse that he had been asked to keep an eye on the nursery for the afternoon.

Death saw the querulous pair off into the park before knocking on Gordon's door to ensure that the house was truly untenanted. He had prepared a cover story for his action should anyone prove to be at home after all, but the house remained deaf to his summons. Satisfied with this result, he made a final sortie to check that Hereward Gordon's parking place was still empty and the coast absolutely clear. With all precautions completed, the would-be thief gently pushed open the Gordons' back gate and slipped silently into their garden.

High in an apple tree of similar venerability to those Death had removed from the nursery garden, old Mr Gordon paused in his relentless pursuit of American aphis and looked down at the intruder below. His immediate reaction was to call out angrily and demand to know just what Death thought he was up to, trespassing in such a brazen fashion, but after a moment's reflection he decided to hold back his indignation and watch which way events unfolded. What Gordon knew, and John Death did not, was that half way along the track he was so blithely following was a refuse pit, dug some six feet deep and with only a covering of fragile brushwood draped across it.

3

Melody, meanwhile, had had her meeting with her union representative, but it had followed a course far removed from the one Peter Gormann had planned. Though prospects had seemed excellent, with the unsympathetic Maggot incapacitated and absent from his role as shop steward, Melody had refused to give an inch from her position of calm acceptance of her fate.

In fact she had gone further. "Mr Wreston," she had charged the union representative when she had grown tired of his constant promises and entreaties to her to change her mind and go along with him. "I don't know who put you up to this, but I didn't invite your attentions, so please leave me alone."

"You could - no I'll rephrase that - you *will* win the case when I present it to the tribunal." Philip Wreston had not survived years of hard fought negotiations without learning to make the most of his gift for oratory, but he'd had a gut feeling from the first that it was being wasted on Melody. "Just allow me to fight this for you and I promise you a result."

"Yes," Melody agreed realistically. "One that'll have everyone in the country sniggering over me. Thank you, but I can live without that."

"And that's your final word?" Wreston asked dramatically.

"It's my *only* word Mr Wreston," she replied flatly.

The union man reported his failure to the Assistant Director (Parks) and his henchman later that same afternoon.

Gormann was feeling unwell. He'd played a brisk game of squash the previous evening and was afraid that he had over taxed himself in his efforts to avoid defeat. Now he felt irritable and under the weather and disinclined to accept any further setback philosophically. He snorted angrily when the union man broke the news that Melody had no intention of working with them. "Do we need him?" He went straight to the heart of the matter with uncharacteristic directness.

"What do you mean?" Wreston stirred uneasily. Alliances with management were unnatural, whatever form they took, and he was a far from happy party to their conspiracy.

"The object of the exercise is to get Death, not Carnforth," Gormann might have adopted the same tone when explaining to a ten year old. "We could still do that by simply leaking the information to the media and leaving them to do the dirty work."

"I'll not be a party to that." Wreston declared stoutly, his worst fears confirmed. "I was prepared to help you, but not at the expense of my member."

"You can't do it Peter." Gormann stared in astonishment as Wilson ranged himself against his superior. "You have to give some thought to Carnforth. This could destroy him if it became common knowledge. Do you really want to live with that on your conscience?"

"If the result meant being rid of John Death, I could live with anything," Gormann stuck resolutely to his guns.

"Well I couldn't and this is one of the situations I stick at. If you go on with this Peter, you do it without me."

"And you'll have the union against you," Wreston added menacingly.

"Well you're a pretty pair of helpmates." Gormann glared malignantly from one to the other of them. "All right, I'll let this one go since you're both so dead set against it. I don't thank you for it though, and you'd best not repeat the gesture too often Gerald, or when I've eventually got rid of Death, I just might turn my attentions to you."

The maintenance co-ordinator flinched at the words, but really he was surprised and relieved that it had all passed off so easily. He didn't know what had possessed him to stand against Peter in the first place, but it might have shown his colleague that he didn't intend to be everybody's whipping boy forever. He did have a mind of his own when he chose to use it and he hoped Peter understood as much from his gesture. He was thankful, though, that he had given in to the other man's insistence that they should both take leave for the period when John

Death would have been under attack. It would give him time to recover from the strain of opposing Gormann. He didn't foresee that it would create extra problems for Arnold Lovett.

4

The park attendant was far from happy with the way that things had gone for him since his appointment. The strong alliance between Simon and Len, though heartening for the morale of the park as a whole, was frustrating Arnold's every attempt to disinter the golden cockerel.

Len was working the first of his rest days now. Ostensibly to cover for the perennially absent George Riodan, though Arnold was convinced a more likely reason was that this restricted his opportunities to continue with his excavations. On the single day of the week when he was free from Len, Arnold found himself under close surveillance from Simon instead.

Not that the treasure seeker ever considered himself to be really free from Len. The eyes of the senior attendant seemed to haunt him whether Len was supposed to be at work or not. Standing at the lodge window, walking through the grounds on his way to do some shopping, Len was never off duty as far as Arnold Lovett was concerned.

He had strolled past Melody and Wreston as they conversed quietly but heatedly. Some men might have thought to linger in their vicinity and strain their ears for a word of what was being said, but Arnold wasn't interested in their problems. He wouldn't have cared if everyone in the park had been masquerading as members of the opposite sex. The newest recruit to the department had absolutely no interest in his fellow workers. His one aim in life was to become the owner of that golden cockerel and he had just had a hint that this might turn out to be his finest hour. Len Saunders had hurried purposefully out of the main gates of the park not ten minutes earlier and now

Arnold was speeding equally purposefully towards what he hoped would be his just reward.

It was a perfect day for digging. A little cooler than the days that had preceded it and after a heavy overnight storm, which had moistened the soil, his efforts should be swifter and less strenuous. With his spade recovered from its hiding place in the bushes, and held surreptitiously down by his side, Arnold set off on his voyage of golden discovery.

A group of cyclists were making their way towards him - a woman, with two children in her wake. Arnold had seen them often enough before and ignored them, as was his policy with all cyclists. This time, however, the situation wasn't quite as usual. Gerald Wilson, on holiday as instructed, was walking slowly along the path behind him, enjoying a stroll in the quiet of the morning. Lovett couldn't afford to have his boss' walk spoiled by such a flagrant breach of the bye-laws. It might infringe on his own activities if he was called to account for allowing it. He flagged down the leading cyclist and politely pointed out to her the error of her ways.

"Fascist!"

There are three types of people who cycle in parks; the favourite amongst attendants being those who immediately dismount from their machines when asked. The ones who feign deafness and continue on their way accordingly can be an irritation, but not as much of one as the cyclists who make up the final group. What no park attendant wants to encounter is the cyclist who is looking for trouble and welcomes a discussion of what needs motivated their choice of employment.

"Put a uniform on some of you and you think you're God."

"Madam," Arnold's mind dwelt unhappily on the success that seemed suddenly to have become just a little more remote from him. "I don't make the rules - I merely enforce them. If council policy is against cycling then I'm obliged to uphold it. I simply follow orders by so doing - I don't necessarily endorse them."

"The eternal cop out!" His antagonist crowed triumphantly. "Every mass murderer from Nazi Germany to El Salvador has bleated that at some time. Don't blame me - blame the other man. I didn't even know the gun was loaded. I'm only following orders.

Don't you ever think for yourself? Don't you ever question what goes on around you?"

"Don't *you* ever get tired of hearing your own voice?" Arnold countered dangerously. "Because I did - about ten minutes ago. You can save your breath and your commie propaganda - I'm just not interested. All I want from you is for you to get off your bike and walk with it as I asked you to do in the first place."

"And if I refuse to I suppose I'll feel a rubber truncheon across my shoulders, or that spade you're brandishing at me?"

"Oh piss off!" A quick glance around had assured the attendant that Wilson was no longer in sight and he had no need to waste any further time on the woman. "I've had enough of you for one morning."

"How dare you speak to me like that in front of my children?" His opponent's air of sophisticated amusement had slipped suddenly, her nostrils flaring with anger. "When their father hears about this he'll...."

"You know who he is then?" Arnold interrupted innocently.

"Mum," a child's piping voice cut through the angry retort welling in the woman's throat as lawbreaker and enforcement agent faced each other across a yard of tarmac, "if *we* can't cycle in his rotten park, why can that man?"

Arnold turned wearily to face a fourth cyclist, who was making an unsteady approach towards their stand-off. "I'm sorry sir," he began the ritual a second time, "there is no cycling allowed in the grounds. You have just passed a notice telling you so."

Warren Hescott pulled up with an effort and slipped rather painfully on to the crossbar. It was his grandson's bike, which he had borrowed when the strain of daily jogging had started to tell on his reluctant body. Cycling was supposed to be an easier form of exercise, but not when the bike is too big for you and the saddle, narrow and uncomfortable to sit on, set much too high. "Do you know who I am?" he responded irritably.

"No I don't. And to be quite frank with you, I don't much care. The sign says no cycling, so you no cycle...Savvy?"

"Young man I..." Hescott began an explanation then, "What are you doing with that spade?" He interrupted himself in alarm.

"I'm making up my mind whether to hit you with it, or to content myself with simply putting it through the front wheel of your bike." The goaded Lovett explained with false serenity. "It seems the only way to prove to the pair of you that I do mean business."

"He won't hit *me* with the spade as well will he mummy?" the second child asked tremulously.

"It's the only way to win an argument a fascist knows," her mother replied gravely positioning herself between the angry attendant and her offspring. "The iron glove and the steel capped boot."

"You've forgotten the rubber bullets Irene," an amused voice cut across the melee and the combatants turned to see Len Saunders watching with a huge grin on his face. "And you should know better than to try to provoke my attendants like that. Hand picked men all of them. Superhuman control? You've never seen anything like it. There's no way you could ever goad one into a quarrel with you.

As for you councillor," Len turned his attention to Hescott as he started to slip away from the fringe of the group, "you ought to know better.

It's him who makes the rules you object to so much Irene." Saunders turned back conversationally to the woman, "He's the fist in the iron glove you were just telling Tracey about.

Come on Arnold," he muttered in a final aside to Lovett, "get yourself out of here whilst she lays into Hescott."

"You know both of them then Mr Saunders?" Len had never allowed his unwanted assistant the privilege of calling him by his christian name.

"Councillor Hescott is the chairman of the Leisure Services Committee which, from our point of view, puts him on a par with God. In the normal course of events he *can* do what he damn well pleases in any of the parks and you're a fool if you tell him different.

Irene is married to Francis Tomlin, a BBC television producer, and a man with a great deal of clout in the area. If you're wise, you take no notice of what she gets up to either."

"Oh come on!" Arnold smiled incredulously. "You mean that I'm expected to stop most people from doing what they don't know any better than to do, whilst not stopping the chosen few from doing what they *do* know better than to do?"

"That's about the nub of it," Len agreed.

"Well I'm not going to do it." The other informed him firmly. "My old man was a lifelong socialist. He'd turn in his grave if he thought I was turning my back on all his principles."

"Then you know the answer don't you?" The senior attendant found it impossible to keep the note of triumph out of his voice.

"Sod off Saunders." Lovett's uneasy temper flared again at the pointed nature of the remark. "Can't you get off my back for *one* day?"

"Mr Saunders to you sonny," came back the uncompromising reply. "And I'll thank you to remember it.

Now, if I can relieve you of that spade you're carrying, you'd best be getting back to your work. Toilet cleaning it's supposed to be isn't it? Well I just glanced in at the Akerman Road toilets. It's what I came back to tell you. In a terrible state they are. Someone's plastered crap all over the ceiling!"

5

Arnold's feelings as he went about the unsavoury task which Len had set him, were not so far removed from Carol's feelings an hour or so later, and for a not dissimilar reason. Inspector Murrow had sent one of his officers to the nursery with the request that Carol return with him to the police station for a quiet word on the subject of the person who had recently been wasting so much police time by masquerading as the felon known as the Middleton Hall Rapist, even though Tom Stone was already under arrest.

CHAPTER FOURTEEN

Peregrine Fitzatherly, maintenance manager of the northern district of the parks division, surveyed the tips of his fingers gloomily as he leaned back in a well-upholstered chair at, what was for him, the unaccustomed venue of Middleton Hall supervisor's office. He was a tall, bony man, with dark hair and a face suggesting good looks run to seed - the brightness of his nose offering a possible explanation why. His habitual attitude towards those around him was one of disbelief that he could have sunk so low. Peregrine Fitzatherly was a man who always tried to take more than he intended to give

Simon Spaulding, in his innocence, had thought that, with John Death disabled by injuries sustained through his tumble into Hereward Gordon's refuse pit, he would be left alone at last to run his area in the manner which best suited him. Already he had set in motion several minor changes he hoped would pass unnoticed on his manager's return. Now it seemed his plans had been no more than wishful thinking. He had returned to his office that morning to discover Fitzatherly sitting at his desk and rummaging through his files, with no apparent intention of giving up the seat to its rightful occupant. The thought crossed Simon's mind, uninvited and instantly rejected, that Death mightn't have the monopoly on bad management practices after all.

"I haven't much time to spend with you," the maintenance manager (north) examined his watch pointedly. "I've wasted a great deal of it already waiting for you to arrive."

"If I'd known you were coming I could have been here." Simon made no attempt to disguise the resentment he felt at the other man's unjust censure.

Peregrine frowned. He had heard of Spaulding's propensity for argument and rancour, and had often professed the opinion that it was time Death brought him to heel. He realised that he had before him a splendid opportunity to show his rival just how that could be done. He raised a languid hand to his brow. "I'm far too busy to keep to an itinerary Simon. I've enough work of my own in the north, without having to run the south as well. Though with management depleted, as it is at present, I've little alternative but to comply with the Director's request and do what I can for you all.

Now – you have a tree planting ceremony coming up soon I believe?" He looked interrogatively at Simon, who nodded. "Councillor Hescott - a v-e-r-y important man. How are arrangements progressing? No - don't tell me!" Simon had opened his mouth to disclaim all knowledge, "John Death tells me that you have it all in hand and that you aren't the man to suffer interference gladly, so I'll respect your feelings and refrain from treading on your toes."

Actually, John Death had been surprisingly frank in his admission, to his opposite number, that all attempts to appropriate the chosen tree had ended in abject failure. In a moment of rare honesty, he had accepted that a personality clash between Gordon and himself prevented a straightforward request for the return of the cedar. He had then tentatively suggested that Fitzatherly, as an outsider, might have more chance of wheedling the tree out of the old man.

The maintenance manager (north) had received the accolade in a manner suggesting acquiescence with the scheme, but was actually planning several steps ahead of Death. The fiasco of an abortive tree planting ceremony in the south would tip the scales of popularity in favour of the north. Allowing Simon to preside over the organisation of this non-event would provide the additional bonus of a scapegoat to take the blame and prove a point to John Death.

Peregrine, of course, intended to drop no hint to Simon of his feelings towards him and remained outwardly open and courteous as he continued. "The ceremony is in," he consulted a small pocket diary, "two weeks' time. The tree is to be a cedar - already in the park I'm told. And you and the councillor have already discussed and decided on the position in which it is to be planted. Excellent! I can see that I shall have no need to trouble myself greatly over your affairs which is, after all, how it should be. Now," he consulted his watch a second time, "the hours are getting away from me so, if you've nothing else to add, I'll be getting on my way. I've three more of John's sites to visit this morning and none of my own attended to yet. Good day to you Simon. Nice to have made your acquaintance again."

Simon watched his departure ruefully. Having no great knowledge of Fitzatherly to warn him, he saw the hand of his own manager in this decision to leave the organisation of Hescott's ceremony to him. Having failed in his own attempts to gain possession of the tree, Death was obviously making use of his enforced retirement from the affair to shift the onus of responsibility for failure firmly onto the shoulders of his subordinate.

"I'll show the bastard." Simon promised himself grimly, as the enormity of his problem gradually sank home. "Thinks he's being very clever and that I won't be able to cope, but we'll see." The thought of appealing to higher management for assistance never occurred to the man. This was single combat between him and his enemy and Simon fully intended the victory should be his – the only problem being how.

2

The subject of Simon's thoughts was, himself, finding life far from enjoyable of late. The fall into the hole in Gordon's garden had damaged his pride almost as much as his body, and the old man's comment whilst helping him out, that it was no more than poetic justice, had given him food for thought. It had been on John Death's own orders that his staff had ceased the tradition of removing Mr Gordon's refuse every week and necessitated the digging of the pit as an alternative method of disposal. It had pierced the armour of the manager's belief in the infallibility of his decisions to lie damaged as a consequence of one.

There was also the business of the phone call to consider. That had been on the first afternoon of his sick leave. Gillian had made it clear in every possible way that she didn't appreciate the extra hours John's incapacity was obliging them to spend together. There had been words between them, she had gone out in a huff, and whilst she had been absent the phone had rung. John had answered it and a male voice, heavy with accent, had asked for Gillian. Receiving the reply that his wife was out shopping, but would be back later, the unknown caller had asked John to tell her that Christian had phoned.

Gillian, of course, whilst inwardly seething at her lover's impropriety in mentioning his name, had denied any knowledge of him. Her husband did not altogether believe her. It didn't take a great mind to connect the name of Christian with a friend known as C, and John had brooded for some days over the unpleasant possibilities the phone call suggested.

His suspicions had developed more solid foundations a few days later. Setting aside any reservations about deliberately eavesdropping on Gillian's conversations, he had gently lifted the receiver of the living room extension when she retired to their bedroom to make a telephone call, "Away from the noise of the television," as she claimed. What he had overheard by so doing had swept away any lingering doubts. His wife was involved in a squalid affair, which had apparently been going on under his nose for some time.

He spent the hours of bitter acceptance undecided what to do. His management colleagues, who admired him as an ideas man and his staff, who feared him for his spur of the moment destruction of their environment, would have failed to recognise the indecisive John Death, who vacillated from one abortive solution to another. Faced with the greatest set back of his life, the man's mind froze and refused to function. The one coherent thought echoing again and again through his agonising, being the need to find a way out of the morass with minimum loss of dignity. But how?

3

Carol had felt she had no dignity left to her by the time Colin Murrow had finished stripping bare her motives for her brief outwitting of the local police. Holding her actions up to ridicule, he had poured scorn on the notion that she had ever really deceived them. Claiming, instead, that they had simply been biding their time before apprehending her.

The Mark II flasher wasn't to know that the inspector was conducting a face-saving exercise. Her experience of the police was limited to childhood admonishments to look up to them as defenders of the weak. She had no way of fathoming how low some of their representatives would stoop in the name of law and order.

It was her pathetic faith in the righteousness of his cause, which probably told in Carol's favour, once the inspector's initial animosity had worn off. Recognising in her a law abiding citizen gone wrong through temporary aberration, rather than a hardened criminal, he was prepared, after all, to make concessions.

Not so Sarah Mackenzie, who was present at the interview and fixed Carol with the most baleful of gazes throughout. Colin Murrow had been scathing in his criticism of Sarah during the early stages of Carol's run and despite it being Sarah's alertness which had led to Carol's eventual apprehension, their relationship had never recovered from the mutual antagonism that had encompassed them. The WPC blamed Carol for the loss of the possibilities Murrow's friendship had once held out to her, but which were now irretrievably lost.

Not that Carol would have had the energy to care even if she'd known. Now that her attempts to fabricate an alibi for her lover had ended in such abject failure, she felt emotionally and physically drained. Grateful too - to the inspector, for no longer bullying and threatening her as he had at first. It was much better to be chatted to quietly, the information being drawn out of her by kindness, rather than by force.

When it was all over, and Carol had escaped with a warning and a word or two of censure, she plucked up the courage to ask after Tom and enquire if it would be possible for her to visit him whilst at the station.

"I'd have no objections to it," the inspector assured her, "but Mr Stone would. He refuses to see anyone, I'm afraid."

"Hasn't he even seen a lawyer?" Carol asked anxiously.

"Not a soul. He just sits in his cell, totally withdrawn from the world. He could be freed on bail tomorrow if he wanted to be, but he won't hear of it."

"You wouldn't oppose bail then?"

"I'd welcome it. We don't like keeping people locked up unnecessarily, and it's doing him no good at all just to sit and brood on things. Unfortunately, our hands are tied unless he starts to take some interest in what's going on around him. There simply isn't anything we can do to help him at this stage."

"Tell him I'm here," Carol pleaded. "Ask him to let me see him."

It had been to no avail and the inspector had returned a few minutes later shaking his head apologetically. Carol made her worried way home and that night had experienced for the first time the dream that was to become a recurring nightmare.

"Prisoner at the bar. You have been found guilty of one of the most heinous crimes ever to be put before me." The voice of the florid-faced judge boomed out across the silent courtroom. "Have you anything you wish to say in your own defence before I pass sentence?"

Standing in the dock, head bowed, looking frightened and desperately alone, Tom remained frustratingly mute.

"Very well then." A murmur ran through the crowded public gallery as the commanding figure in the scarlet robes lifted the ominous square of black material and, with great deliberation, placed it carefully on his head.

"No!" At the rear of the courtroom Carol was being forcibly restrained by Inspector Murrow. Then she awoke from the horror and faced up to what she knew she must do.

"I want to see Tom Stone." She informed the duty sergeant when she arrived at the police station. It was her fourth port of call that morning. Already she'd been to her bank, the post office and her building society.

"I explained this to you before Miss Trennick," the inspector seemed a shade less understanding than he had on their previous meeting. Carol wondered if his sleep was also being troubled in some way. He spoke sharply, not taking the time to smile. "Mr Stone refuses to see anyone."

"Inspector Murrow," a new Carol looked back at him unflinchingly, "I intend to see Mr Stone, and both you and he had better make up your minds to that. If I have to camp on your doorstep for a week first, so be it. But I *shall* see him." There was a determination about her the policeman recognised and responded to.

"Very well Miss Trennick," he acknowledged the situation gracefully. "We'll put your ultimatum to Mr Stone and see if it changes his point of view in any respect. I make you no promises mind, but if I were him I think I'd take the easy option and see you." The smile, which crinkled at the corners of his mouth, warmed his face until he turned to the stony-faced policewoman standing at his shoulder.

"Sarah," Murrow glanced back at her with marked distaste, "do you think you could manage a cup of coffee and a biscuit for a visitor - or is even that beyond you?" The tall girl left the room without a word. When she returned with the refreshments, Carol could see by her red and puffy eyes that she had been crying. It seemed a very unhappy police station, the waiting woman reflected idly.

"I never done it Carol!" It had taken several hours of persuasion before Tom had been induced to relinquish his stand and come to the interview room. His entry had been hesitant and his manner restrained. For a long while they sat facing one another across the table, the only communication between them being when Carol placed her hands over his to halt their continual clasping and unclasping. It was something she had been expressly forbidden to do - to touch him in any way - but the constable deputed to watch them wisely turned a blind eye. That was when Tom's reserve had finally broken. Weeping unashamedly, he looked up into her face, his eyes no longer afraid to hold hers. "I promise yer I never.

I was in the park waitin' to see yer. Been 'angin' about there for days on the chance. Then this geezer runs past. I don't know who 'e is, do I? Didn't take much notice of 'im at all until 'e drops somethin' at me feet in passin' - at least I thought at the time 'e'd dropped it, but now it seems 'e played me for a mug an' threw it. I'd just gone into a crouch to eyeball the gear – an 'ood with some sort of paintin' on it - when I looks up, an' finds I'm surrounded by…. You don't believe me do yer?" He stared searchingly into her eyes.

Carol stirred uncomfortably. The story had a painfully familiar ring to it. "Of course I do Tom," she protested. "Go on with what you were saying."

"You *don't* believe me Carol!" She fought, without success, to free her eyes from his. "You wanna know 'ow I know? It was when the ol' bill told me what yer done 'cause of me. Dressin' up an' pretendin' you was who they thought I was so they'd let me go. I kidded meself at first that at least one person believed I was innocent, then the penny dropped. You was doin' what you was doin' 'cos yer thought I was *guilty,* not 'cos yer thought I was innocent. You wanted people to think the rapist was still around, even though I was banged up in 'ere. It never crossed yer mind for a moment that that was 'ow it was anyway.

I want out." He rose to his feet and addressed the young policeman trying hard not to eavesdrop on the couple.

"Tom." Carol held out her hand imploringly. "What am I supposed to believe? What about the things they found at your house? The books? The women's clothing? What about them?"

Stone turned at bay. "Well, what about 'em?" He answered question with question. "Me private life's me own innit? It certainly don't concern you no more. But think on it. I've seen books like that described as educational and what 'arm can there be in lookin' at educational books? Wishful thinkin' never done no one no 'arm. As for the clothes – well there's no cause to 'ide that from you no more. Belong to me wife, don't they?"

"Your wife?" Carol's wail of anguish startled the pigeons from the window ledge outside. "You haven't got a wife!"

"Take me down John." Tom turned to the policeman again.

"I've paid your bail Tom," Carol pleaded.

"I never asked yer to." He spun back savagely.

"And I've instructed a lawyer to defend you."

"Despite you think I'm guilty? Now why do that?"

"B-Because I love you," she faltered.

"Love me?" He repeated incredulously. "Your love mean you'll stand by me whatever? You keep it! There's enough people out there already wot finks I done it. What I'm lookin' for is the one who's goin' to stand by me 'cos they fink I'm innocent. To me, love is trustin' people enough to believe what they tell yer. Your kind of love," he shook his head sadly, "you can stick it!"

"Up on the notice board with my picture?" She asked quietly, but it was too late, he'd already gone.

The desolate figure, who stumbled sadly from the police station a short while later, bore no apparent relation to the formidable woman who'd stormed it a few hours earlier. There was little left for Carol now. Bail for Tom had taken what savings she had and the price of his lawyer had been a second mortgage on her home.

She smiled ruefully to herself as she remembered how much her house and the few comforts it contained had meant to her. Now she had transformed it into a financial millstone around her neck and still Tom questioned the reality of her love. How little he knew, she thought bitterly, as she turned the corner of her street. How little he knew.

CHAPTER FIFTEEN

Mid-morning at Middleton Hall and a tap on the door of Simon's office was followed, almost immediately, by Len Saunders looking in. "Sorry." He noticed Peregrine Fitzatherly lurking in the corner and nodded briefly in his direction. "I'll come back later."

"If you wouldn't mind Len," Simon smiled equably.

Fitzatherly scowled. His scheme to discredit Spaulding, and through him Death, was not progressing as planned. Fate, in the shape of Peter Gormann, had knocked the cedar tree firmly back into his court.

"Oh Perry." Gormann was not long back from his spot of leave and the news of John Death's downfall, which everyone was intent on being the first to report to him, had been no less welcome for its being second hand. The Assistant Director (Parks) much preferred the sophisticated Parks Maintenance Manager (North) to the devious Parks Maintenance Manager (South) and at most times was prepared to shower him with favours not even hinted at to the other man. The long drawn out saga of Councillor Hescott's tree, however, allowed for no such concessions to be granted. Potter was involved and would be bound to see that heads rolled if the issue was fouled up in any way. Though not wishing to strike a sour note with Fitzatherly, Gormann was obliged to put his position before the man in a clear and succinct manner.

"I've left all that to Spaulding," Peregrine explained impatiently when the cross-examination was over. Fitzatherly in no way reciprocated Gormann's feelings towards him. In fact he considered him to be little better than John Death, who he detested. Gormann's single virtue in the eyes of the Parks Maintenance Manager (North) was his seniority and therefore his degree of influence over Fitzatherly's fortunes. But for that, the latter wouldn't even have given him the time of day.

"Is that wise?" Gormann regretted his introduction of the note of censure, but it was unavoidable under the circumstances. "He isn't exactly noted for his supportive attitude towards us you know."

"You think that I should take a closer interest in Spaulding's organising of the ceremony?" Peregrine faced up to the inevitable.

"I think that you should take the role from him," Gormann replied firmly. "He isn't a man we can trust to do his best for us. Too much is riding on the ceremony being successful for us to take the chance."

Fitzatherly had found things at Middleton to be pretty much as he had left them at the end of his first visit there. The sole difference being that, thanks to Gormann, he was now considered to be in the driving seat and it was as important to him that all should go well as it had been to his colleague Death. Peregrine had decided that a tree of suitable size and similarity to that held by Gordon should be purchased. Not for him the chance of a humiliating rout by the old man. He had just broached his opinion to Simon, who had replied that Hescott would easily see through that one, when Len Saunders had interrupted by looking in at the door.

"It's my decision." Peregrine declared pompously when the senior attendant had gone.

"And your neck too." Simon had added - but not out loud.

Fitzatherly had little else to say and had taken his departure of Simon shortly after. Len, who had obviously been waiting for that moment, slipped back into the office almost immediately.

"What's up with Fitzy?" He enquired conversationally. "Have you been upsetting things again?"

"Not this time." Simon laughed and went on to recount the latest episode of the cedar saga.

"Everyone's been so busy planning to steal the thing," Len summed up the situation succinctly. "Has anyone actually considered *asking* old Gordon for it?"

"You think he'd give it to us after what Death did?" The other asked doubtfully.

"Perhaps not," the attendant acknowledged, "but surely it's worth a try. He's such a contrary old bugger, he might just give it to you out of pure cussedness."

"Well you'd better ask him. I'm not about to risk a flea in *my* ear."

"I might just do that," the originator of the theory agreed thoughtfully. "Still, that's for later. What I wanted to see you about now was Melody."

"Melody?" Simon repeated blankly.

"Melody." Len was guilty of a mild sarcasm. "You remember her? Used to work here a while ago. Lad who thought he was a woman."

"All right Len. There's no need to be so heavy-handed about it. I know who you're talking about. I was surprised at you bringing the name up, that was all. I thought she'd left us."

"That's just it," Saunders hesitancy, so at odds with his usual bull-at-a-gate approach, was unexpected, "she hasn't."

"Oh," Simon prompted gently, marvelling that Len could be capable of what in anyone else he would have taken to be embarrassment. "Why not?" He nudged again when the older man seemed loath to continue.

"I suppose," Len chose his words carefully, "it's because she hasn't got anywhere else to go. She was down on her luck when she came to us. We failed her. Now she's just bumming around."

"That's a bit unfair Len." Simon reproved him gently. "She chose that way of life for herself. The rest of us can't be expected just to break step and fall in with her."

The attendant's eyes narrowed. "You're entitled to your opinion I suppose Simon. But you're wrong. No one would *choose* to be the way Melody is. That's why I've always felt sorry for her, and hadn't the heart to tell her to get on her bike when she started to drift into the park in the evenings. I know what it's like to get a raw deal from life - I've had a few of my own in my time I can tell you. Even so, I didn't bargain for having her following like a pet dog wherever I went. It got so I couldn't do my work properly and there was always the fear of Lovett saying something I'd have to take him up on. In the end I suggested that, if she needed to talk to someone, she came round to see me at my Lodge after work.

I know," he met Simon's critical eye with a rueful shrug of his shoulders. "I'm a fool - you don't have to tell me that - but I *do* feel sorry for the kid and I *am* the only friend she's got left. I couldn't just abandon her as everyone else did.

It would have worked out too - if she'd only been content with that - but I expect you can guess what happened next?"

"She thinks she's in love with you?" His confidante hazarded.

"Something like that." Len admitted. "Love's too strong a word for it I hope, but she's certainly reading more into what I've done for her than I ever intended to be there."

"I suppose it's only natural," Simon ruminated. "For her to see you in that light I mean."

"That's what bothers me," Saunders contradicted flatly. "It isn't bloody natural. Not between Melody and me. She's too young for one thing and she's a bloke for another. Whatever doubts she might have on the subject, I don't share them. She's no woman, and that's a fact!"

"And that's precisely why none of the rest of us wanted to get involved," the younger man pointed out. "No one could afford to. People like Melody have to be left to sort out their problems themselves as best they can. It's hard, but it's self preservation. Now you'll just have to find a way out for yourself. Couldn't you go away somewhere for a week or two and give her a chance to get over it? You must have holidays owing to you."

The senior attendant kicked out angrily at the base of the filing cabinet. "And give Melody a final nudge over the edge you mean? How can I do that to her?"

"You'll have to put her straight about your relationship sometime Len," Simon summed up his companion's dilemma. "The longer you leave it, the harder it will be on both of you."

The older man sighed. "You're right, of course, Simon but...oh hell!" He stared silently out of the window, lost in unfathomable thoughts until Simon broke in on with one of his own.

"Has Melody tried medical treatment at all?"

Len shook his head. "She won't even consider it. Afraid to face a doctor, I suppose, and I can't really blame her for that. It's a hell of a thing to face up to anyway, without all the additional traumas of surgery to contend with."

"Long term though Len, it's probably the only way."

"Probably," a shrug of the shoulders acknowledged Simon's logic, "but who looks at long term when it's today their world's falling apart?

Still," he sighed again. "I suppose I'd best get back to harassing Lovett. I've wasted enough of your time already with my problems."

"It's what I'm here for."

"Yeah," the other nodded unhappily and in a moment a still more troubled supervisor was staring gloomily at a closing door and reflecting on the latest in an apparently endless sequence of problems.

2

John Death, who as a rule had very little in common with Simon Spaulding, was at that moment experiencing a fellow feeling of endless doom. Despite serious misgivings about the venture, he had closed his mind to reason and set out to spy on Gillian's latest liaison with C.

It had been difficult for the man to continue to behave within the family unit as if he didn't know that his entire world was coming apart at the seams and though his pride choked on the need, he felt he had, nonetheless, carried it off well. The fact that his wife paid him so little heed had helped. The occasional slipping of the mask he wore to face the world easily passed unnoticed by someone who seldom looked at him anyway. Gillian, he was sure, knew nothing of his suspicions about her affair.

Wednesday night had been fine. Death had deliberately put the car into a garage for a protracted overhaul the day before in order that his wife should have no chance to borrow it. It would be so much more convenient to shadow her on foot, or on public transport. Though the remaining aches and strains from his adventures in Gordon's garden still troubled John and made walking painful, he gritted his teeth and struggled on. Cap pulled down low over his eyes, dark glasses set firmly on the bridge of his nose and coat with the collar turned up despite the warmth of the day. He was so close behind Gillian as they boarded the bus that he could have reached out and touched her if he'd tried. The impulse to do just that and have it out with her there and then gripped him for a dangerous moment. He held on tightly to the stair rail to stop himself from obeying it, and the bus driver irritably ordered him to pay up, or get off and stop blocking the bleeding gangway. Obediently dropping the correct coins into the receptacle at the driver's elbow, Death had made his way to the seats at the downstairs rear, where he could best watch the exit unobserved. Gillian had gone upstairs.

Christian was all that John had feared he would be. Everything that he himself unquestionably was not. Tall, blonde and depressingly handsome, he had an extrovert personality, which sent shock waves of popularity reverberating around him wherever he went. Worst of all, he was demonstrably affectionate to Gillian by means of constant looks, touches and verbal caresses. After an hour of discontented observation of the couple via the mirror behind the bar of the noisy riverside pub to which Gillian had led him, her husband was feeling dispirited and afraid.

Death stuck it until ten o'clock and then decided that he couldn't take anymore. There was, in any case, no point in his prolonging the unhappy experience. He needed no further proof of his wife's infidelity and every moment he spent in their unconscious company increased his own feelings of inadequacy to deal with what was going on. Why was he content to secretly observe them? Why didn't he simply stalk across to their table and tell Gillian that he was taking her home? The answer to both questions was Death's overwhelming fear that revelation of his knowledge would result in the conclusion of his marriage, rather than the end of the affair.

Would that really be such a bad thing though? He surprised himself with the thought. Now that he knew about this, could he ever be happy in her company again? Probably not, but was he going to allow another man - and a *foreigner* at that – to have the final say? Death shook his head firmly. Gillian must be brought to her senses and made to see reason. The question being how?

3

Gerald Wilson would probably have wondered why his immediate subordinate should spend his time worrying over the luxury of a wife who wanted to leave. The problem besetting the maintenance co-ordinator was the complete opposite of the one besetting John Death. Gerald Wilson was bedevilled by a wife who wanted to stay.

Not that Mrs Wilson simply wanted to stay with her husband. Gerald could have coped with that. Eileen was someone he loved after a fashion and to whom he had grown used over the years. What was tearing the guts out of Mr Wilson was that his wife wanted to stay at Middleton Hall.

The prolonged leave on which Peter Gormann had insisted in order to avoid the aborted Melody Carnforth crisis had been a double-edged sword so far as Gerald Wilson was concerned. His panic at the thought of being away from his duties hadn't just been because of the amount of work that would build up on his desk during his absence - papers to be signed, plans to be formulated, requisitions to be authorised and the like (already his headache was becoming more savage as he enumerated all that awaited him on his return) – his greatest fear was of being away from the worry for so long he would find it impossible to return.

That wasn't to suggest that Gerald Wilson was afraid of work. Far from it. Give him an engine to strip down, or a chassis to spray, and he would be at it for hours. Many years earlier he had trained as a mechanic, served an apprenticeship in a garage and been happy in his work. If it hadn't been for that accident to old Baxter, and a wife with ambitions beyond his peace of mind, he might have been enjoying it still.

Baxter had been the foreman of the workshop in which Gerald had made a pleasant living when the days of his apprenticeship were still recently behind him. The accident had been caused by an insecure hoist and when the old man had been carried off to hospital in an ambulance Warner, the manager, had looked around for someone to take his place as a temporary measure. His eyes had rested on young Wilson. The lad had fitted the bill, filled the gap and become a permanent replacement for Baxter, who unhappily succumbed to his injuries only days after they had occurred.

Even this might not have been the end for Gerald, though he always associated the loss of his peace of mind with that day the hoist defaulted. Life as workshop foreman was still tolerable, for a while he was still able to set off for work with a whistle on his lips. It was only later that, softly and perniciously, ambition began to grow in Eileen's mind.

The extra money Gerald was paid for being foreman had been very useful when setting up home after their marriage. It purchased luxuries they would not otherwise have been able to afford. It was when Eileen became pregnant and had to give up her own job in consequence, that she began to brood over how little money her husband actually brought home.

The bleak thoughts dominated the bloated days of her confinement. She crooned rhymes about the inadequacy of it to the gurgling baby in the pram she pushed ahead of her through the weeks of post-natal depression. Gradually, as their children grew, she browbeat the reluctant man from one better paid job to another, forcing him to progress steadily up the ladder of success.

Wilson wasn't sure how it came about that he changed course in mid-stream and become a horticulturist. He had been a fairly keen amateur gardener as a younger man, even working an allotment for a month or two, but his technical knowledge of the subject was somewhat restricted and his experience of running a parks department was precisely nil.

It had been at the time of Potter's initial purge on taking over the directorship of Leisure Services that Gerald had applied for the position of Senior Workshop Technician - servicing the lawn mowers and other machinery used by the department. Somehow - and he could never offer a satisfactory explanation for it - he had been passed over for that, but had found himself taken on as Gardens Superintendent instead. It was worrying of course, and his headaches increased dramatically with his acceptance of the post. The salary was similar to that of the job he had really wanted, however, and he was so afraid of facing Eileen and admitting failure that he took the job, and his first faltering steps into the unknown.

The months passed and Wilson muddled along. He didn't do his job badly considering his inexperience, but the grass in his district was generally out of control and most of the shrub borders shrouded in weeds. When the time came for the second reorganisation of Potter's term of office. someone suggested that it might be wise for Wilson to be moved from a post with which he was so patently unable to cope. The opinion was taken up and Gerald was promoted to Maintenance Manager (North).

The headaches worsened. Insomnia became a real problem. Wilson awoke from an uneasy sleep one night to find he was suffering violent pains in his chest, later diagnosed as symptoms of stress. He discussed with Eileen the advisability of finding a less demanding job, but she pointed out that the children needed new school uniforms, he had promised to buy a new car that summer, her sister Julie had just bought a television with a larger screen than theirs, the.... When the latest (to date) Potter purge was declared Wilson applied for, and was appointed to, the position of Parks Maintenance Co-ordinator, second in command of the Parks Division. Eileen celebrated the appointment by throwing a small party for selected friends. Gerald celebrated it with a second ulcer.

He realised he had passed the point from which there was any going back for him now. Eileen enjoyed his status too much for that. She especially enjoyed living in the grounds of Middleton Hall, which she was coming to look on as the family estate and describing as such to her friends. Not even in the most optimistic of his dreams could

Gerald imagine Eileen allowing him to give up the smallest part of what she had driven him to achieving. She would be bound to make his life a living hell is he so much as suggested it.

Wilson was still brooding over the quality of his existence when Mr Gordon passed him in the park. The two men nodded, but that was all. The Gordons and Wilsons didn't socialise. The old aristocracy and the nouveau riche of the department had no common ground on which to meet.

Gordon was on his way to see Simon Spaulding. Despite his personal problems, Len Saunders had found the time to have a quiet word with his former boss about the dispensation of the cedar tree. The idea as put to him by Len had appealed to the old reprobate's sense of humour and he was quite prepared to part with his treasure so long as the rewards for his generosity were acceptable.

There was no real fear of them being otherwise. A startled and effusively grateful Simon didn't even try to counter the bartering prowess of his unexpected saviour. All he could do was to stammer his grateful thanks, agree the concessions, and stare ahead of him towards the faint pinprick of light at the end of his tunnel.

CHAPTER SIXTEEN

Len Saunders stormed across the nursery yard - bursting into the supervisor's office without stopping on ceremony. "That bloody Lovett!" He exploded. "I'll swing for him one day! I don't know how he managed it but he's done it just the same."

"Calm down Len," Simon Spaulding admonished him, looking up in amusement from the papers he was sorting. "You'll have a seizure the way you're carrying on."

"I'd like to seize on that bastard's scraggy neck!" The senior attendant remained as tightly wound as a spring. "You know what he's done don't you?" He leaned forward on the desk, breathing fire and fury over the amused Spaulding and gesticulated incoherently in the general direction of the park. "He's only dug that bleeding hole again. It's back there as large as life this morning. Grinned at me as I cycled past. I nearly fell into the bloody thing in surprise. You'll have to do something about him this time Simon." He paused in his diatribe to take in gulps of air and the other man took the opportunity to offer an explanation.

"Lovett didn't dig the hole this time Leonard. It was dug by Henry, on my instructions, because that's where I've decided that Councillor Hescott's tree should go." He smiled at the attendant.

"Oh." For a moment Len stood looking foolish and deflated as the wind was taken from his sails, then a beatific smile spread slowly across his face. "Does Lovett know yet?" He enquired hopefully.

"I haven't told him."

"Then I think I'll go and find him and just walk a little way with him in that direction." Saunders turned to take his leave of the office. "I can't miss the chance of watching his face when he sees what you've done to him. Quite Machiavellian that," he applauded as he left.

"Len." Simon called him back. "Have you done anything about Melody yet?"

The attendant's face sobered. "I told her we'd best stop seeing each other," he admitted. "And I spelled out to her exactly why."

"How did she take it?"

"I don't really know. She said she could see my point of view and understood my feelings, but then she went very quiet, and clammed up for the rest of the evening. I haven't seen her since."

"How long ago was that?"

"Two days. Why?"

"Oh I don't know. I've felt guilty about her since you said we'd all let her down when she was here. I suppose I'd like to have my mind put at rest by hearing that she was doing fine. Selfish to the end you see?" He smiled wryly at the other man. Len shrugged his shoulders unhelpfully and took himself off without another word.

Simon turned back to his papers with a sigh. The resurgence of his good fortune had filled him with the desire to help others as he went about the world. Even Maggot, pale and shaky and weighing a stone or two lighter, had been greeted with concern and offered an easy ride for a day or two until he was completely recovered. A chance he turned down ungraciously. The sullen malcontent had brooded at length through the days of his incapacity and had worked up the suspicion that Simon might have been somewhere at the root of what had befallen him. There was nothing he could seize on as proof, but Maggot was sure enough in his own mind to refuse sustenance from the hand he felt had bitten him.

The supervisor really didn't mind. He had more to turn his thoughts to than the uncorroboratable suspicions of his old antagonist. More to turn them to than the day's ceremony even. The point on which the young man's thoughts were centred lay several miles away from

Middleton. He had received a phone call from Christine the night before.

Not asking him to come back to her. Christine would never be as open and upfront as that. In fact, as phone calls went, some men might have found it far from satisfactory. Simon knew his lover well enough to see through the veil of unavailability in which she shrouded herself, however. To him the fact she had phoned at all could mean only one thing. He was back in favour again.

"Barry's gone." The woman announced dramatically, once conversational preliminaries were over.

"He's left you again?" Simon failed, marginally, to keep the triumph out of his voice.

"For the last time." Christine's voice hardened as she interpreted the other's tone. "There's a limit to second chances, and I think Barry and I reached it this time."

"Oh?"

"Don't get me wrong though Simon," she interpolated hurriedly. "This isn't an invitation to you to return to our old ways. Those days are gone forever. I'm only telling you this because I felt I would explode if I didn't talk to someone about it."

"What about the boys? Aren't they good listeners?" Simon goaded a little, with an assumed tone of bored disinterest.

"They don't live here any longer," Christine replied coldly. "Barry thought it was time that they went out into the world and learned to fend for themselves."

Simon, who had long been of the same opinion, smiled to himself. Barry had certainly shaken up his wife's insular world during their brief reunion. He became aware that Christine was still running on.

"I'll always be married to him Simon. You know that. In my mind; if not in fact. There's no way anyone else could mean as much to me. You understand that, don't you?"

Simon actually understood three things. Christine's husband had left her - apparently for good this time. Her sons had finally escaped from home and would no longer be around to cramp his style once he and their mother resumed their relationship. Christine was holding out an olive branch towards him and asking if he still wanted to be friends. She could couch the truth in whatever way she fancied but that was the reality of it and that was the belief on which he intended to base his responses.

"I'm a woman who values her self-respect. I couldn't bear for anyone to consider me cheap or easy. Do you find that strange? Do you think I'm easy?"

"I think you're bloody hard work most of the time. Worth it though. Give me ten minutes. I'll be over to show you just how much I've been missing you."

"Simon!" The anticipation in her voice told Simon that things were okay between the two of them again. Putting down the phone, he hurried off to change.

2

Sammy the dog sniffed thoughtfully. Since his last visit there, a tree had appeared on the lawn at the rear of the Hall. One he had, at first, welcomed as an addition to the quota in the grounds. Investigation had proved it to be rather too spiky for his purposes, however. He raised a leg tentatively but recognised that he must stand so far back from the tree to avoid irritation that there was no way he could reach it, however direct his aim. He growled in annoyance and looked around for a means of relieving his feelings.

A figure was approaching in the distance, a spade resting casually on one shoulder. Sammy was aware that it couldn't be his friend Peter, because that favourite human had taken a fortnight's holiday and wouldn't be back until the following week.

"Hello Sammy." It was Henry who greeted the scruffy mongrel by tugging at his tail in passing.

The animal ran a black nose across the offended item to check it for damage and then wagged it half-heartedly. He recognised Henry as a friendly human he was prepared to allow a few liberties, but he was far from being one of Sammy's favourite people.

Watching for a few moments as Henry began to scoop soil from around the base of the tree, Sammy reflected that humans were certainly strange creatures in the ways they occupied themselves. Dig a hole, fill it in, dig it again, fill it in again and so on and so on for months on end, without ever finding so much as a chicken bone. Eventually they plant a tree in the hole, but not one that could be of any utilitarian value to a dog, and hardly has it been installed before someone else is apparently digging the thing up again. He scratched at a flea behind his left ear and snorted disgustedly.

Henry, having removed enough soil to make a reasonable heap for Warren Hescott to formally replace in the hole, set off in search of the silver spade, which was to be used in the ceremony. Sammy probed the heap carefully before marking it for future reference, then set off on a tour of the woodlands. Somewhere in the park, he reasoned, there must be a jogger or a cyclist on whom he could vent his spite.

3

"Stupid waste of time." Studying his reflection in the mirror, Warren Hescott found himself dissatisfied with what he saw.

Not that the elderly councillor was in any way unhappy with his physical appearance. It was the collar and tie embellishing it he objected to. That, and the suit hanging on a doorknob in the background, innocently serving to heighten his irritation.

The old man had suffered a recurrence of his earlier misgivings concerning the festivities at which he was supposed to provide the focus of attention. His original opinion, that the passage of so many years was best left unremarked and unrecorded, had reasserted itself. He found himself objecting, both to the idea of the ceremony, and the need for him to give it some credence by attending amidst a group of people for whom he had very little time.

He was especially annoyed that his ruse of insisting on that one particular tree had rebounded on him so resoundingly. Who would have believed that old Gordon would part with the thing so easily after cherishing it for so many years? Certainly not Hescott. It only went to prove what he'd always maintained - the man was a humbug and not to be relied on in any way.

"Damn it. Why should I go?" Warren demanded of his reflection, but needed no reply to know the answer. He was a councillor. He was chairman of the Leisure Services Committee. It was expected of him. Hescott was familiar with all the reasons, but resented them none the less for that. He examined himself for the cause of his disinterest and realised, suddenly, that he had become old and bored with the dreary routine of life. The councillor who had fought so many elections on the ticket of being, 'the man who cares', found, unexpectedly, that he no longer did.

"All right my friends," he addressed himself to the organisers of the official tree planting ceremony. "I'll lend you my support this time because I promised it and I never renege on my word. It's the last help you're going to get from me though - and I won't wear this!" He tugged at his tie. "Nor this." He tore at the buttons of his shirt. "And I'm certainly not going to wear a suit for your edification."

Councillor Hescott had enjoyed a thought that justified his position as a member of the Leisure Services Ideas Committee. It was stunning - but so simple it quite took his breath away. He *would* attend the ceremony, but would kill two birds with one stone by getting his exercise for the day as he journeyed to the Hall on his grandson's bicycle. The brilliance of the scheme left Warren feeling quite rejuvenated. He whistled as he went off to check the tyres.

4

Unaware of the councillor's views on the commemoration, the various dignitaries began to drift into the Middleton Hall gardens shortly after 2pm.

Isaac Sharpe of MAPS (Middleton Area Preservation Society) was amongst the first to arrive; accompanied, as usual, by a mousy little middle-aged woman with a shrill voice. Mr and Mrs Sharpe paid no heed to the beauty of the clusters of virginal white flowers on a tall Eucryphia across the lake from where they were standing. Nor did the scent of fresh mown grass wafting from the plantation of young trees in the woods in any way delight their senses. The official policy of MAPS was to ignore anything about the Hall that didn't fit in with their oft-repeated views that the gardens were in a state of total neglect. The park could be ablaze with colour, the grass neat and trim; still the members of MAPS, coached by their leaders, were able to close their eyes to what they had no wish to see. It was a mark of the influence of the group locally, that most articles written about the gardens at the time included, somewhere, a denunciation of the borough for failing to maintain a more satisfactory standard. It was against this background of deliberate blindness, that the Sharpes stood discussing the tree in disparaging terms.

"So small! It hardly seems worth the planting."

"And what a position for it. No one will even know it exists."

"Very suitable my dear. Bearing in mind who it commemorates."

Pause for laughter.

"Typical of the park though."

"Typical - and yet, in another way, untypical my dear."

"How so Isaac?"

"For them to do any planting at all."

"How very astute of you Isaac. We must bring that up at one of our meetings."

"We have my dear - many times. Ah, here's Mrs Konan."

Avril Konan, president of FOM (Friends of Middleton), greeted her archenemy warily. "Isaac, how good to see you. And you've brought Anne with you." The two women brushed cheeks in the semblance of a kiss.

"Avril my dear; you grow younger each time I see you."

"Is *this* the tree?"

Sharpe pursed his lips. "I'm afraid so."

"But it's so small. It hardly seems worth the bother of planting."

"That's what I was saying to Isaac. No one will even know it's here,"

"Very appropriate, since it's for Hescott." Pause for laughter. "Ah, here come Potter and his cronies."

The Director of Leisure Services strode along with a brow like thunder. He considered the entire affair to be a, "Load of bluidy nonsense," he would have left to Gormann if it hadn't been for the Blacks Meadow redevelopment project he was still trying to push through committee. Needs must though, and he was there on sufferance, but very unhappy about it. He greeted, "the smarmy Jew boy an' that ould cat Konan", with as much pleasure as he could feign under the circumstances.

At his chief's side, Gormann, quite frankly, was worried. Being unable to raise Hescott on his phone and ascertain what time the councillor intended to arrive at Middleton, he had been forced to play things by ear. As a consequence, the tree planting had been set for a time agreed at a brief meeting several weeks earlier, but never actually confirmed during the interim.

The Assistant Director (Parks) wouldn't have minded so much if there was someone on to whom he could shift the blame, should the affair warrant it. Wilson, however, having returned from his holiday, had immediately succumbed to a fit of depression and was now absent on sick leave. Death had returned from sick leave, but only that day, so could hardly be considered accountable for anything which did or did not happen during it. Fitzatherly had, very wisely, decided to take his holidays to coincide with the ceremony and any aftermath there may be. Spaulding was there though; Gormann ruminated with a lightening of spirit. He had been involved from the beginning and would be ideal to take the brunt of any blame. The danger, of course, was that he was becoming type cast in the role and care would have to be exercised to ensure that he had no opportunity to complain of victimisation. He consulted his watch again. Damnation! Where had that old fool Hescott got to? He was six minutes late already.

5

Hescott was finding the going considerably more difficult than he had expected. He had taken his grandson's bicycle for quite a long spin the previous day and hadn't realised until he mounted the machine on his way to the ceremony just how chafed his buttocks were in consequence. Really, he couldn't imagine how young Kenny stood that painful saddle; and stood was truly the operative word, for he dared not sit down and suffer the discomfort the act of so doing induced. It was the uncomfortable necessity to stand on the pedals, which decided the old man to forsake the roads and main paths along his route to the tree planting, and travel cross-country instead. By taking Ferry Road to the Gibbs Lane entrance to the park he could cut through the woods, up the hill to the high path, pass the Cascade at the head of the lake and glide gently down the slope to where the infernal tree planting was to be carried out. Thus saving himself at least a mile of agony.

6

Sammy, angry at the absence of his friend Peter and at having his tail pulled in such an undignified fashion by Henry, was lying in wait in his favourite ambuscade in the lee of a regenerating elm stump to the north of the Cascade. The day had been a boring one so far. Only a mother with a baby in a pram and two men with dogs too large for Sammy to tangle with had passed since he had stationed himself there. He was scratching idly at a flea on his right flank and wondering whether to cut his losses and make for home when a sound, still in the distance as yet, made him suddenly stiffen, his body alert, his tail swinging slowly.

7

Simon and Henry had stationed themselves near enough to everyone to be on hand should any emergency demand their presence, but far enough away to avoid the complaint that they were overhearing conversations not intended for their ears. They were the first to observe the approach of Councillor Hescott. They watched with astonishment, which gradually became amusement, (tinged with concern for his future in Simon's case) and then unbridled hilarity, as Hescott, leaning low across the handlebars, his legs rising and falling like pistons, propelled himself desperately down the hill from the Cascade. A small blur of black and brown fury streaking at his heels.

Potter, Gormann and Death were fortunate enough to be able to step to one side as their guest of honour swept past them. The Sharpes and Avril Konan were not so lucky.

Still pedalling furiously, Hescott might have been able to avoid them all, if his leading wheel hadn't driven itself deep into the heap of soil so thoughtfully positioned by Henry. The front of the bike stopped dead, the back reared up and the councillor continued on over the handlebars; coming to rest on Isaac and Anne Sharpe, who dragged Avril Konan down with her as they tumbled into total chaos.

CHAPTER SEVENTEEN

The bitter attack on Simon, which followed the demolition of the guests at the tree planting ceremony, began once the ambulance had taken Warren Hescott and the Sharpes to the local cottage hospital. Avril Konan enjoyed a morbid fear of such places and had refused point blank to be taken there, so Carol, in her role as nursery first aider, had been called on to treat her instead. Despite the break in proceedings all this brought about, feelings were still running very high when the post-mortem finally got under way.

Only Potter declined to wait around and hear the bones of the affair picked clean. Henry swore later that the director had laughed out loud as Hescott landed with his arms around Mrs Sharpe's shoulders and his knee in her husband's groin. Gormann had been shocked to see his chief patting Sammy, who had hesitated uncertainly on the periphery of the pandemonium he had caused, and call him a "bluidy guid dog."

The truth was that Potter was feeling light headed and was afraid to stay for fear his exuberance might seem out of place. The Leisure Services Committee meeting, at which his plans for Blacks Meadow were to be discussed, was scheduled for that same evening and it was obvious that Hescott, the one stumbling block to the unopposed adoption of his scheme, would now be unable to attend. No wonder the man was whistling quietly to himself as he hurried off in the direction of his car. He might well have leaped into the air and clicked his heels together if he hadn't had his dignity to consider.

Gormann, of course, had no way of knowing what was going on in Potter's mind and, assuming the senior man to be working himself up into one of his furies, was frantically sifting around for a means by which his scapegoat could take the blame. He had already assigned the role to Simon, what was worrying him was the terminology by which the charges could be brought. How *did* one blame the supervisor for the actions of a stray dog in his park? It was John Death who proved the ally of the Assistant Director (Parks) for once, providing him with the background information necessary to his case.

"That was the dog we spoke about once before, wasn't it Simon?" Death's voice was casual, his eyes narrowed and his brain alert.

"It was Sammy," the supervisor admitted reluctantly.

"I thought I issued a firm ruling then, that the dog was not to be encouraged in any way."

"You did," Simon agreed.

"And?" The maintenance manager probed patiently.

"And what?" The other decided to go down with all guns blazing. "It was Councillor Hescott who was encouraging it, so far as I could see, *and* breaking the bye-laws into the bargain, by riding a bike through the park. It's something that's getting to be a habit of his lately. Perhaps it's time someone in higher authority had a word with him about it."

"John." Warned by a snigger from the interested Henry, Gormann intervened swiftly. "I think this conversation would be best continued in private, don't you?"

"Simon has an office." Death bowed to the authority of the younger man.

"Simon?" Gormann turned to the supervisor.

"This way." With a heavy heart, the latter accepted the inevitable, and was marched away like a prisoner under escort.

For all the extra privacy the four walls of Simon's office gave the trio they might just as well have continued their business out in the open. As the echoes of their exchanges rang out across the nursery garden, an interested knot of gardeners began to find plenty of jobs to do within earshot of the office window.

In the end, it was left for Hescott to decide. Gormann, at least, could see that there was going to be no easy victory over Simon and overruled John Death, who was pressing for instant suspension. He decreed that Simon's future should rest on what attitude the councillor adopted towards the affair. Big trouble from Hescott would lead to the adoption of Death's suggested course. A mild complaint would mean it being overlooked this time.

Gormann delivered his edict and left the park impressed by his own sense of justice and fair play. Death and Spaulding went their separate ways united in the belief that Gormann had gone for a cop-out. It was an aggrievement that was still on Simon's mind as he made love to Christine later that night. It was an irritation, which might have troubled Death through sleepless hours, if more startling events hadn't erased it completely from his mind.

2

Gillian had never really intended her estrangement from her husband to go as far as it had. She had been aware of John following her from the moment she boarded the bus, slightly ahead of him, the evening she set out for her liaison with Christian. The knowledge that she had been found out had surprised her at first, for she hadn't believed John to possess either the interest, or the intellect, to make the discovery. Realising that his presence was proof that she had underestimated him, however, she became first frightened, then excited at the prospect of having to find a way out of her unexpected dilemma.

Mrs Death considered her problem calmly. With only five stops before she was due to leave the bus; she had little time to make plans. Admittedly there was always the option of simply travelling on past her intended destination, but she baulked at that solution as a stopgap unworthy of her devious mind.

The plan she finally adopted occurred to her just after the fourth stop. She would take no action to prevent John from following her. Would lead him straight to Christian, allow him to study the opposition for a while, then bring the affair to an end before his eyes, without the watcher ever knowing she had been fully aware of his presence all the while.

It was a plan filled with subtle strengths and possibilities. Let John see the sort of men she could pull if she had a mind to and he might well consider the advisability of leaving her so much on her own. Let him see she was a woman who could take men up, or drop them without a second thought, as the fancy took her. Best of all, it would bring to a satisfactory conclusion an affair which had been becoming increasingly distasteful to her of late.

It might have been Gillian's age beginning to tell on her, or simply a manifestation of her growing boredom. Surreptitious meals in second rate restaurants and squalid moments of sweaty sexual climax in Christian's seedy flat had seemed exciting once. Now she found herself longing for a quiet, uncomplicated life. She had visions of days spent hoovering, or washing dishes. Perhaps a little gardening carried out during fine weather. She had dreams of evenings spent sitting at home watching the television, or burying herself in a good book. Gillian felt she'd had the wild fling and the quest for lost youth. She was ready now to welcome middle age.

It was the discomfort of being tied up one evening, which had finally convinced her. Gillian had never been one to fantasise on being taken by force and the indignity of Christian's use of her for that purpose had made her start to look more closely at their relationship. The rope burns, which had taken so long to heal, had been the turning of the tide in her husband's favour. John might be boring, but he was very safe. She had already made up her mind that she had to break with Christian. Her husband's discovery of the affair had simply brought that termination forward.

Seeing Christian from her newly revised viewpoint, that evening, she was unable to explain to herself why she had ever considered the man to be attractive in the first place. His face was much too Nordic, his teeth too perfect and his body too slim. John, she remembered with sudden affection, had a comfortable lived-in look, much more attractive than the hungry sensuality of her lover. Nor was John forever pawing at her body. She shook Christian's questing hand away and risked a glance to establish whether or not her husband had noticed her rejection of the other man's advances.

The briefest of looks was enough to show her that her plan and the harsh realities of life were going their separate ways. John was no longer there. Convinced by all that he had seen, that his marriage was no longer a viable concern, he'd left several minutes before.

Gillian brooded over that. It wasn't the way she'd intended things to work out and she experienced a vague panic at the deviation from her scheme. How typical of John to foul things up in that fashion. He was supposed to remain to hear her exit line. How else was he to know that she'd returned to the straight and narrow from which she'd wandered? Without a word of explanation or goodbye, she rose determinedly to her feet and set off in pursuit of her marriage.

3

Days passed, Gillian studied her husband covertly at every opportunity but John gave no sign of the secret knowledge they shared. Gradually the woman became afraid. How could he remain so outwardly unchanged? How could he continue to conceal the way he felt behind a mask of normality? Was he involved in some deep scheme of his own? Or did he simply not care? The unanswered questions buzzed round and round in Gillian's mind until, from the depths of her sleepless and foodless wretchedness, she conjured up one last brilliant idea.

Her seduction of her husband was gentle but overwhelming. The bemused man, returning angrily from the aborted ceremony and its resultant contretemps with Simon, found himself swept into a world pleasured with experiences of which he had no previous knowledge. Gillian's affair with Christian had taught her many ways of satisfying a man. She experimented with her favourites on this opening night of the second stage of her marriage. So devastating was her success, that her husband was obliged to give work a miss the following morning. He might have managed to get there, rubbery as his legs were - the old John Death would have done - but Gillian, in her total domination, would allow him only one quick phone call before she reached for him again.

4

If Carol had known how easy Gillian was finding it to put her love life back on an even keel she might have reconsidered her own way of trying for the same result.

She had bailed her Tom to his freedom from the police cells. The best barrister her money could afford was preparing a case for the defence, based on the monosyllabic responses to his questions, which were all he was able to prise from an unhelpful client. Tom should certainly have been grateful for all that Carol had done for him. He should have thrown himself at her feet and thanked her for standing by him when no one else wanted to know but, on the technicality of a turn of phrase, he refused to forgive her for what he saw as a failure to believe in his innocence.

Carol could probably have lived with that. She had a lifetime's experience of ungrateful recipients of her ministering. What was twisting her into knots, by the futility and mindless stupidity of the gesture, was the way the aggrieved Tom spent his time hanging about in the grounds of Middleton Hall.

"Tom!" She had exclaimed in horror, encountering him in the woods as she was making her way home one evening shortly after his release from custody. "What on earth are you doing here?"

"It's orl right Carol," he had laughed bitterly, "I ain't on duty. Left me 'ood an' tracksuit at 'ome today, din' I?"

"Don't be a fool!" Fear for him had made her angry. "What are you doing here Tom?"

"Waitin'," he had replied laconically.

"For me?" Her heart had lightened in the hope of reconciliation. "That's nice of you Tom."

"For the rapist." He had shattered her hopes with deliberate brutality.

"I don't understand."

"No," he had looked her up and down disparagingly, "I don't suppose you do. You'd 'ave to believe in me innocence 'fore you could see what I'm about. Never mind though – I'll put you in the picture just for old time's sake. You see, I ain't 'im."

"I know that Tom." Carol had put in quickly, but been ignored.

"Now I know it, an' 'e knows it, but we're about the only ones 'oo do. Not that I blame people for that I suppose - well not all of 'em anyway," he had shot a sidelong glance at his companion, "so I thought to meself Tom, I thought, what you've got to do to prove your innocence is to get to grips wiv the real one. I mean, if the two of us can be seen togever in the same frame like, then they got to admit one of us ain't 'im. Even you'd 'ave to allow that Carol."

Ignoring the innuendo in her lover's words, the latter went straight for the weak point of his reasoning. "But Tom, supposing he attacks again whilst you're in the park and the police don't catch him? If they think you're him now, something like that would only confirm it for them. Be sensible. Keep right away from here until he's safely behind bars and you're in the clear."

"Sorry Carol." He had shaken his head and strolled off along the path, leaving the woman's dreams of a future with him balanced on the brink of oblivion.

5

Carol often saw Tom hanging about around the park after that. Sometimes he would be loitering in the shade of the sweet chestnut glade, where early nuts the squirrels had rejected crackled underfoot. On other occasions he might be sitting on one of the benches at the back of the Hall, feeding the pigeons. Sometimes he would be standing on the bridge where she had first encountered him, staring moodily into the dark waters below. They didn't speak to each other and if Tom even noticed her he made no sign. Carol could tell though, with all the intuitiveness of a woman in love, that he was becoming more and more desperate as the days passed and the man he was waiting for steadfastly declined to expose himself to the public eye.

Had he done so he might well have chosen for his victim the slim, blonde figure who frequented many of the same quiet areas of the grounds as Tom Stone did, but there he would have been wasting his time.

Melody would have had little to offer if he'd struck. The lonely girl was beginning to believe that she had little to offer anyone anymore.

The break with Len Saunders had hit her hard. She had told the unhappy man that she understood why he shied away from a deepening involvement with her - and so she did. Unfortunately, her understanding the reason behind it did nothing to deaden the pain she felt at this latest betrayal of her by someone in whom she'd thought she could trust.

In Len, Melody had believed she had at last found someone with genuine feeling for her, and the courage to stand up and tell the world he didn't give a damn for its censure of her. She hadn't been looking for the kind of love the senior attendant feared. What Melody sought was warmth and affection from someone – anyone. In an uncaring world, she was becoming as desperate as that. Her family, Billy Danton and now Len, had all offered incomplete hope, which left her more damaged than ever when it wasn't realised. Frightened and alone, rejected by the God whose sick joke on her seemed totally without purpose, Melody had become as isolated as it was possible for a person to be.

6

Len, alone of those who noticed the gaunt ghost haunting the grounds, guessed something of what the girl was being put through, but like Carol with her Tom, was unable to help in any way. He worried though, far into a succession of sleepless nights and it was as a result of a particularly disturbing train of thought during one of these sessions that he finally made up his mind what had to be done.

Simon agreed obligingly enough when the attendant came to him and requested a few days holiday at very short notice, but the cloaked query as to why Len was taking them was gently brushed aside. Saunders had no wish for anyone else to know where he was going. Far from certain that what he was doing was the right thing, he had no intention of risking dissuasion by discussing it at this formative stage.

Having to leave Melody on her own was particularly worrying to the man. Even though she would no longer speak to him, he could at least keep an eye on her comings and goings to see that she came to no harm. There was no alternative though. He could hardly ask Lovett to carry on the surveillance amongst all the other extra duties Len had dreamed up to keep the attendant busy during his absence.

Arnold hadn't greeted the news he was to be free of his tormentor for a few days with any degree of enthusiasm. His hopes for his hole having been dashed by Simon's decision to have the Hescott cedar planted in it; there was no benefit for him in being alone. Len's division of their duties was far from fair, in Arnold's opinion, but at least he did clean *some* of the toilets and clear *some* of the litter. With the senior man absent, Arnold saw the superfluity of unpleasant tasks stretching out before him in a parade of unremitting tedium.

It was a pleasant change then when, on the second morning of Len's absence, Arnold was the one to find a body hanging from a lower branch of the magnificent Cedar of Lebanon, which dominated the back lawn of the Hall.

CHAPTER EIGHTEEN

Councillor Warren Hescott was limping slightly as he took the steps of Middleton police station more slowly than usual. The effects of his tumble from his bike were still troubling him and making long sessions in the council chamber especially trying to the man.

He was so stiff! It was as well the bike was too damaged to ride anymore. He doubted if he would even be able to swing his leg across the saddle at the moment. The quack at the hospital had recommended a total relinquishing of his civic duties for a week or two, but Hescott had never been one to take things easy. The public were funny animals in that respect. Let them suspect for a moment that you weren't giving your all on their behalf and they could snuff out your career like a candle at the next election. The councillor didn't want that to happen. His idea that he was growing tired of the endless grind of problems and debates had proved to be no more than a temporary aberration; probably caused by over tiredness as a result of too much cycling. Councillor Hescott had decided to give up the bike and return to gently jogging around the lake at Middleton Hall as soon as he was able.

He had held his local 'surgery' at the church hall as usual that evening. Warren liked to believe that local people found him approachable whenever they had a problem. Once a month he made himself even more available. Having an evening when anyone could come to him with a problem he would do his utmost to unravel.

One of the problems put before Hescott on this occasion had concerned the arrest and subsequent release of Thomas Stone.

A former landlady of the unfortunate man had tut-tutted happily over the fall from grace of her erstwhile lodger and discussed his peculiarities at length with her friends. Her indignation, on taking a short cut home one evening, and seeing him hanging about the grounds of the Hall in a manner that made her fear for her safety, was deep. Bringing the matter to the councillor's immediate attention, she had wrung from him a promise to visit the police station and establish the reason for the villain's continuing freedom.

Warren Hescott was extremely touchy about anything concerning Middleton Hall just then. If Simon Spaulding's continuing employment there really depended on Hescott's attitude towards him, he might as well start studying the 'jobs vacant' columns without delay.

The councillor looked around him furtively as he came out of the church hall and, having established that he was unobserved, slipped a dark brown Balaclava helmet over his head. He wasn't sure whether he was more self-conscious of the bandages, which still swathed his head as a result of his accident, or the woollen hat he was obliged to wear to protect them from the vagaries of the weather. On the whole, he thought he preferred the bandages, but the quack had been insistent that they required protection. The Balaclava had been the only hat he could find flexible enough to accommodate so much padding underneath. With light drizzle falling, he had to wear it and make the best of a bad job.

Colin Murrow had dealt firmly with the councillor's complaint. Telling him that Mr Stone was as innocent until proven guilty as any other criminal at present out on bail. No, the police had not opposed his freedom. They considered the reputation of the notorious felon to have been greatly embellished by local folklore and did not believe Mr Stone presented a threat to anyone. Even so, it was certainly unwise of him to loiter in the grounds of the Hall under the circumstances, and the appropriate Home Beat officer would be instructed to have a word with Stone about it in due course.

Councillor Hescott was not really satisfied with Murrow's explanation but he had to be content. Though officially an independent, he leaned towards the right in his views on crime and punishment, and believed kid-glove treatment of criminals was directly related to an increase in crime. He mocked the idea that Tom had simply picked up the hood when someone had thrown at his feet. He had no belief in a story that the man had then panicked when he saw the police and run. The councillor snorted. Innocent men did not behave like that. He would have something to say about this laxity on the part of the local force at the next full council session.

"Middleton Hall is on your beat isn't it Sarah?" Murrow addressed the tall redhead he encountered as he made his way towards the canteen shortly after Hescott left.

WPC Mackenzie had just come off duty after a long and tiring day at court, followed by an extra duty helping to police a local CND rally. She flinched visibly at the question, much preferring the inspector to ignore her altogether, than to feign ignorance of facts with which he must be fully cognisant. "Yes sir." She answered formally; striving not to betray her agitation.

"Tom Stone has taken to hanging about the gardens there since his release. You remember Mr Stone of course?"

"Yes sir." How could she ever forget the man whose arrest had been the peak before the trough in which her career now floundered? Or that poor woman who had done so much for her lover; only to be so unjustly treated by him in return? Stone she had no sympathy for. He had doubtless deserved all that he got but - what was her name? - Carol Trennick was a different matter.

Sarah had got over the bitterness she had directed at the person whose antics had led to the breakdown of a promising relationship with Colin Murrow. Carol was, after all, a woman and as such could be more easily forgiven.

WPC Mackenzie was saving all her disapprobation for the opposite gender. She had discovered men to be creatures without honour; not to be trusted or admired in any way.

"I'll speak to Sergeant Bentley on the subject and appraise him of what I'm telling you. I want you to have a few words with Stone and point out to him the error of his ways. Nothing threatening or abusive, of course. Just a gentle nudge to show him we know what he's up to and don't approve. Okay?"

"Yes sir." Sarah seldom uttered more than those two words to Murrow anymore. What else was left for them to say? It had been her ready use of them, the night of the party, which had put her in the professional backwater in which she was now becalmed. It was by the use of them now that she marked time whilst she looked for a way out.

WPC Mackenzie had grown up a great deal during the past few weeks and the naive girl from the country, whose sole driving force had been an ambition to arrest a particularly squalid criminal, had vanished without trace. Her education in the pitfalls of real policing had been swift. Her only regret was that it had probably come too late to save her career.

2

Simon Spaulding was issuing instructions for the day's work when Arnold Lovett broke in on him with the momentous information that someone had hung themselves from one of the trees in the park.

"Anyone we know?" Even Maggot was prepared to brighten perceptibly at the thought of another suicide. The last had been some fifteen or sixteen years before, as he and Jack Higgins jointly recalled. A young girl had hung herself from scaffolding against the walls of the Ionic temple. Her ghost was reported to dance on the terraced lawns whenever there was a full moon in summer.

"John Death?" Tom Hollins put in hopefully.

"Or Carol's funny fellow?" Henry came closer to home.

"Not Melody?" Simon was struck by a sudden concern for the absent Len Saunders.

Arnold had more or less recovered his breath by now and was full of his role as bringer of important tidings. He reflected on the clamour of questions for a tantalisingly long time. "It's a stranger to me." He admitted at last.

"Are you sure?" Arnold scowled at Maggot for asking.

"I'll just go and check on that." Henry put the view of the silent majority into words. "Arnold's probably got it all wrong."

"It was most likely a golden cockerel perched on a bough he saw; not a suicide at all." Jack Higgins brought a laugh with his po-faced comment.

"Okay." Simon decided to take command of the situation. "That's enough jokes to be going on with. Now, I want Arnold and Henry to go and stand guard over the body, whilst I telephone the police. The rest of you go and have a look at it if you want to, then get off to whatever you should be doing, but keep an eye open for the public, and try to fend them off from going along that particular path if you can. Don't tell them why though, or we'll have a crowd gathering around the fellow."

It was ten minutes or more later before Simon had succeeded in getting through to the police station with the news of Arnold's grisly discovery, and then telephoned the civic offices to leave a message about it for John Death, who had apparently not yet arrived at work. This done, he hurried out into the park, as interested as anyone in being privy to whatever was to be seen.

The sight greeting his eyes when he reached the cedar was of the body of an unshaven and untidy young man, dressed in blue jeans and cagoule, dangled from a low growing branch. His heels, no more than four inches above the ground, rested together above a double impression in the soil, made when the unfortunate had miscalculated his initial attempt at suicide and had to shorten the rope and jump again.

"Where's Lovett?" Simon addressed himself to Henry, who was standing on his own studying the figure with interest.

"I told him I could manage without him. He went off to clean the toilets."

"When I want you to countermand my orders, Henry, I'll ask you to." Simon said evenly. "Now, *I'll* stand guard over this poor devil whilst *you* go and look for something to cover him with when we cut him down."

Across the lawn, unnoticed by her former workmates, Melody looked on despairingly. She had been sleeping rough in the park for several nights now and had been the first to find the body; even before Arnold Lovett came on the scene. So totally unexpected had it been, the girl had stared at it in fascinated horror for some time before she was able to break the spell and back away. That had been an hour or more ago and ever since she had somehow seemed to see her own face superimposed on that of the suicide whenever she pictured him in her mind.

Melody was growing frightened. She knew that she was nearing the end of her tether so far as resilience to her propensity for misfortune was concerned. The sight of that morning's suicide had seemed somehow to indicate to her an ultimate solution - if only she had the nerve to carry it through.

The lone figure of Simon Spaulding was beginning to take an interest in his surroundings and was looking this way and that for any indication of members of the public who had slipped through his protective net. Melody decided that it was time for her to melt unobtrusively into the background. Her clothes were creased and damp from the overnight drizzle and she brushed at them unhappily with a grubby hand. "Oh God!" She mouthed a prayer despairingly. "Show me a way. Show me that this isn't all there is ever going to be to life."

"Hello." A soft voice spoke unexpectedly behind her. "What are you doing hanging about here at this hour of the morning?"

Melody wasn't to know it yet, but that meeting with Sarah Mackenzie was to be the turning point in her life.

3

John Death scowled when he read the scribbled note left in the middle of his desk; one corner weighted down with a heavy ashtray. It was the fact that it had been logged at 7:45 which most annoyed him. There had been a time when he could be relied on to be at his desk by 7am at the latest and available to deal with any early morning emergencies. A successful marriage might be made in heaven, he mused to himself as he crumpled the note and tossed it petulantly into his wastepaper bin, but a successful career could only be forged in the office.

The renaissance of Death's marriage had got off to a glorious start; but had lost its impetus of late, for all Gillian's enthusiastic sexual prowess.

The trouble was that John was not a very sexually oriented person. The highs and lows of his life turned on his successes at work rather than in the marriage bed. Carrying through a scheme which everyone had told him was impossible could bring all his senses to a climax mere copulation could never achieve.

The truth was that he was not a married man by nature. He had sought a wife purely and simply because he believed that to get to the top he had to conform. Successful executives had wives to accompany them to business functions and dinner dances. A bachelor, on the other hand, was always suspect.

John had never considered love as a reason for marriage. Sex had simply been the way to produce the one or two children that gave the impression of a settled home life to employers seeking to fill a vacancy for a reliable man. It was not an entertainment, nor even a pleasure, especially when it interfered with the smooth running of his career. He resented Gillian's preoccupation with it for causing him to be late for work three mornings in a row. It would have to stop, he told himself, as he made a second unsuccessful attempt to contact Middleton Hall by telephone. His wife must be made to see that this carnal craving of hers went unreciprocated by him and must be curbed.

Actually Gillian didn't need that fact to be spelled out to her by her husband. It had not escaped her notice that he was not enjoying their sessions together anywhere near as much as she did. His constant complaints about headaches and excuses that he was tired were beginning to try her patience a little too far.

The previous afternoon she had, in fact, taken a train ride into the city and strolled along some of its seedier streets. The dingy clubs, pornographic film parlours and blowsy women, with which they abounded, interested her. She had thought that she'd had enough of Christian's strange practices and was ready for a more settled way of life, but now she wasn't so sure.

Life with John was steady to the point of boredom and Gillian knew she needed more than that. She decided to investigate the city more thoroughly. The possibility of putting the things she had learnt from Christian to a practical use excited her. It would certainly be better than wasting them on an unappreciative husband. She sang happily to herself as she chose the clothes she would wear for this latest adventure. Gillian always looked forward to a new challenge in life.

4

Carol Elizabeth Trennick, on the other hand, did not enjoy any sort of challenge. That facing her a few days later least of all. It was one she had already taken up too recently to be easy with, especially when remembering how ignominiously she had failed to carry it through.

And yet Carol Elizabeth was fully aware she had to stand up this second time and be counted. To do what she felt a woman had to do. Not so much for the simple principle of justice, though it was at stake here, but the point where that principle of justice applied to Tom. She may have looked on helplessly as he fashioned a rope for his own neck; she was not prepared to stand by whilst he went on to pull the noose tight. In Carol's mind Tom and the recent Middleton Hall suicide had very much in common - the only difference being that the latter was already dead.

The unhappy man had ignored the warning administered to him by ex WPC Mackenzie - Sarah had quit the force the day after encountering Melody - on behalf of Inspector Murrow. Stubbornly continuing with his set plan of apprehending the real flasher and thereby proving his own innocence to the world. He could not, or would not, take note of the possible pitfalls, which made his chosen path so dangerous.

Carol left the nursery by the back gate and made her way towards her bench by Repton's bridge as usual that dinnertime. She was aware that Tom Stone kept an eye on her movements whenever she was in his vicinity; in order to effect a strategic withdrawal should she try to venture too close; and she had no wish to frighten him off at this stage. Not wanting an involved game of hide and seek before she could come to grips with him, the woman had decided to lull her prey into a false sense of security. Following her usual pattern of behaviour, she did not intend deviating from it until he was off guard and easier to apprehend.

It was a plan that pleased Carol, who hadn't been aware that she was capable of such low cunning, and it worked surprisingly well. The unsuspecting Tom saw her safely to her usual seat before turning his attention to the woodland paths, which were the favourite haunt of the flasher. His mind thus preoccupied, he didn't know Carol had crept up behind him, until she startled him by taking a firm grip on his arm.

"For pity's sake Tom!" Carol implored. Her hold on him tightening for fear he should consider flight before she had got out all she wanted to say. "Give this up whilst you still have the chance. If that man attacks whilst you're in the park you're done for. Finished!"

Stone turned on her angrily, a cruel retort welling in his throat. Then the sincerity in the other's plea struck home. He swallowed the hurtful words thoughtfully. There was no denying that Carol had given her all for him, going far out on a limb despite his ingratitude. It obliged him to make concessions. "I thought I told yer Carol," he answered reprovingly, "I gotta prove me innocence somehow. I can't 'old me 'ead up again until I do."

"But Tom, the police have warned you and I've begged you. Can't you see that you're wrong? You're simply playing into the real rapist's hands by hanging about in the park so much. I don't understand why you're being so stubborn about it. If everyone else can see the stupidity of what you're doing, why can't you?" Her fingers dug into her prisoner's arm in emphasis and he winced at the pain.

"Everyone else don' 'ave to live with what I'm livin' with now, do they?" Tom looked earnestly into his lover's eyes.

"But it won't go on forever Tom. The trial will prove ...."

"Nothin' at all, so far as I can see." He interrupted bitterly. "Oh don' think I'm not grateful for what you done for me by puttin' the readies up front for a brief an' all. I *am* grateful an' I *do* thank you for it, but even if 'e gets me off it'll still 'ang over me 'ead 'til I'm pushin' up daisies I might o' been the one, an' only got off 'cause I 'ad a good brief.

I gotta catch the geezer what really done it if I want people to believe in me innocence. I gotta. It's the only way. You must see that Carol."

Carol could see nothing of the sort. All she was sure of was that her man was set on destroying himself for no reason at all and she was facing an unacceptable future without him. "Oh Tom," she tried without success to tear herself free of the eyes that held hers and stemmed her eloquence through their soulfulness. "It won't work. You won't prove...."

"What was that?" Her companion interrupted, turning his head to one side.

"What was what? What Tom?" She repeated urgently when he didn't reply.

"Hush." He waved her to silence. "There. You must 'ave 'eard it that time."

Carol had certainly heard the scream, which had risen tremulously, then broken on its highest pitch. It had originated somewhere in the woods close at hand and the blood in her veins had run cold at the sound of it. She turned to face the danger, as another scream echoed more loudly than those preceding it, and was taken off guard as her lover made a sudden lunge in that direction.

"Tom." She maintained her hold and tugged him away from the continuing cries. "Tom." She repeated soothingly.

"It's 'im - the rapist. It must be."

"Then stay here in the open where everyone can see you." Carol implored him.

The man shook his head determinedly. "I said I'd 'ave 'im, an' that I'm gonna do. Now leave go of me Carol." He shook himself free of her restraining hands as a further scream set the pigeons scattering from the stag-headed monarchs of Chestnut Square, "We can't 'ave 'im gettin' away!"

"Oh Tom!" Carol's despairing moan was lost in the swish of the returning undergrowth, as Tom Stone crashed through it towards the echoing proof of his innocence.

CHAPTER NINETEEN

Arnold Lovett stood looking out across the lake towards a plethora of waterfowl exuberantly gulping down the bread being tossed to them by a woman and her child on the opposite bank. His eyes, seemingly taking in this tranquil scene, belied a mind in turmoil. His fingers toyed with the sharp edges of an envelope in his trousers pocket.

It was funny, Arnold's face twisted in bitter sweet amusement at the admission of such a weakness, but he had never thought the place would come to exert such a hold on him that leaving it would seem a terrible wrench. In the poignancy of the moment, even Len Saunders didn't appear quite such a despot to the reflective attendant.

That wasn't to pretend that Lovett wasn't glad Len was far away from Middleton and unable to make capital of the situation. The attendant was a resilient young man, but there would be something in the triumph of brute force over intelligence, which he was sure would bring him down. After all, Saunders had gone out of his way to be as obnoxious as possible in every theatre of the war between them and would be bound to enjoy the reason for the eventual parting of their ways.

Not that Arnold could really blame Len for that. And since the senior attendant was not the reason for the notice of leaving, which Lovett intended to present to Simon Spaulding later that day, the attendant could afford, in the end, to be magnanimous towards his implacable foe.

It had been an item of news featured in most national newspapers the previous day, which had robbed Arnold of a reason for remaining at Middleton Hall. The attendant could remember the paragraphs almost word for word. Their dispatch of the hopes and dreams, which had driven him through adversity for so long, would be emblazoned on his memory forever:

RUNAWAY DOG GETS THE BIRD

Farmer John Jacobs (42) was angry when his five years old Jack Russell terrier, Spikey, chased a rabbit across a field on his farm at Concton, County Durham yesterday morning and refused to return when called.

John, seven years a trumpeter in the local brass band, followed his pet, named after entertainer Spike Milligan - a Jacobs' family favourite - and found him firmly fixed half in and half out of a hole he had dug in the side of Wilyns Wynd. A prehistoric burial mound situated in the corner of one of the Jacobs' fields.

Farmer John, a former sergeant in the parachute regiment, admitted that he had to take a firm hold of his temper as he fetched his spade to enlarge the hole and free his errant dog. His ill humour was short lived, however, when the first cut of the tool revealed a gleam of gold beneath the surface of the soil. Subsequent investigation revealing it to belong to the much sought after golden cockerel buried by Francis Herries, author of 'The Clasp', within the text of which clues to the whereabouts of the buried treasure were hidden.

The reports went on to describe the reactions of hider, finder and family to the discovery; and in one or two cases to discuss the morality of the use of such an important historical site for such a contemporary purpose. The writers' rhetoric was wasted on one reader though. For Arnold, there was no life after the loss of his cockerel. Not one worth living anyway.

The fact that the cockerel had been found several hundred miles away from where he had been convinced it was hidden hadn't fully communicated itself to Lovett yet. What was concerning him most at this stage was the injustice of some simple northern swede basher benefiting from such a stroke of good fortune at his expense. It really

wasn't fair. Arnold could have accepted his loss more
easily if the farmer had at least been looking for the thing.
The fact that he hadn't, made the attendant's subsequent
loss of fame and fortune so much more galling to bear. He
was brooding darkly on the iniquity of it all when the sound
of screaming erupted suddenly into his conscious mind.

Arnold's reaction was immediate. For all that Len
Saunders thought of him, the attendant was no coward, and
in his present embittered state of mind actually welcomed
trouble as a means of relieving his tensions. Stopping only
to take the lock and chain from a nearby gate to use as a
weapon, Arnold ran in the direction of the continuing
screams, his eyes alight for battle.

2

The felon the press had dubbed the Middleton Hall
rapist turned this way and that in front of the full-length
mirror in his bedroom and studied his reflection critically.
The new look he had adopted wasn't quite what he had
hoped it would be, he decided at last, but it would have to
do.

Having just returned from a fortnight's holiday on
the Costa del Sol he was completely unaware of Tom
Stone's unfortunate predicament. If he had been he might
have taken the chance to fade quietly into obscurity, instead
of going for the new image he was about to introduce.

Inspector Murrow had got it right when he had told
Councillor Hescott that he didn't consider the man who
haunted the darker corners of the grounds of Middleton
Hall to present much of a threat to anyone. The man
himself would have been the first to agree.

Certainly the title of rapist had been unfair on a timid
and inadequate fellow, so frightened of women that his
only contact with them was the occasional exposure of the
lower portions of his trunk from a discreet distance. It had
been the sudden infamy and the notoriety that went with it

had led him to abandon his original comfortable raincoat for the sleeker tracksuit and hood he now wore. Making him toy, for a while, with the idea of living up to his reputation, until the thought of the physical involvement that would incur had made him think again.

He *had* decided to do *something* about his image, nonetheless. The painted hood he had dumped on Tom Stone had always tended to make him somewhat claustrophobic behind the inadequate eye slits and permanently snarling mouth. A Burt Reynolds film he had seen whilst on his holiday (dubbed into Spanish but the message had been clear) had convinced him that a more macho image was called for. An account, in a magazine, of SAS activities in the Middle East, had shown him the form this machismo should take.

The pity of it all, when he came to do something about it, was that his foreign adventure had left him rather short of ready cash and unable to afford a complete new wardrobe of khaki battledress and appendages. It was disappointing, when he was so keyed up for change, that all he could afford was a Balaclava to replace the hood, and a long dagger he had no intention of using; but which was similar in appearance to the one hanging from the hip of the soldier in the photograph he was using as a pattern.

He subjected his reflection to a final critical examination and remained dissatisfied with it. A navy blue tracksuit and a khaki Balaclava were not at all what he'd had in mind when the heat and the alcohol of the Spanish resort had combined to suggest this adopted course of action. He was almost prepared to wait a while before appearing in Middleton in his new disguise, rather than expose himself to ridicule by looking neither one thing nor the other. Reluctance to waste the afternoon sitting in front of his television decided him on making the best of a bad job, however. So he pushed the Balaclava into the top pocket of his tracksuit, where it bulged alarmingly, and jogged off towards the park.

3

Jane Cummins was on her way home from the supermarket, her shopping bag full of purchases and her mind full of how she was going to bulk them out into a satisfying meal for a family of five growing children and an ever-hungry husband, when she was suddenly confronted by the man whose alleged exploits she had been reading about over her breakfast cereal a few weeks earlier - the Middleton Hall rapist, in all his sartorial splendour. There was no denying that Mrs Cummins was impressed by her assailant's new look; especially the dagger he used to slice through the handles of her shopping bag in an uncharacteristic moment of whimsy. Her screams were prolonged and came from the heart.

4

Tom Stone was the first to appear in response. He burst into the clearing, where he saw Jane screaming at the cowering flasher, who was poised for flight; but *thought* he saw Mrs Cummins cowering from the Middleton Hall rapist, who stood threatening her with a knife.

Tom wasted no time on considering his best course of action. With a cry of raw triumph, he flew towards his adversary, caught his foot in a trailing bramble, and tripped and fell headlong onto the dagger, which the frightened flasher had completely forgotten he had in his hand when he turned to face the onslaught of this fearsome foe. With a grunt of pain Tom collapsed, clutching his side. The blood, which bubbled darkly from between his fingers, offering the vociferous Mrs Cummins fresh reason to scream.

5

Arnold Lovett's approach had been more carefully thought out than Tom's. Not for him the hopeless charge against the artillery of a superior enemy. He had spied out the lie of the land from behind a protective veil of undergrowth, marked Stone's attack and its inevitable outcome, then fallen on the rapist from behind, swinging his lock and chain like a medieval weapon of war.

His quarry, already reeling from the cacophony of sound emanating from his ill-chosen victim and sickened by the steady trickle of blood from the body of his would-be captor, was taken completely by surprise when a hard metal object struck him a numbing blow across his hand. The dagger slipped from his fingers and was lost in the long grass at his feet.

Disarmed and shaken, he turned to face an Arnold uttering intimidating barks and cries of excitement as he advanced remorselessly, lock and chain whirling dangerously above his head.

The attendant was enjoying the means he had found of ridding himself of the frustrated anger he had felt since reading about the discovery of the golden cockerel; but his reluctant opponent was not. Eyes wide with fear, he turned and fled into the undergrowth, leaving Arnold in command of a clearing in which Jane Cummins, her energy expended, could now only whimper quietly to herself and Tom Stone bled steadily into the pool of dark liquid spreading slowly beneath his body.

6

Simon Spaulding stirred in his sleep. Something had disturbed the man, but not enough to waken him. He altered his position and the book, which he had been reading before nodding off over his sandwiches, slipped from his lap to the floor with a thud.

The sound brought Simon back to the world with a start; but so heavy eyed and slow witted from sleep, that it took him several moments to recall where he was. He sat up, scratched his head languorously, then looked around in amazement as the door of his office flew open and crashed against the wall.

A dark haired man looked cautiously into the room. Heavily moustached, slightly balding, he studied the recumbent supervisor with suspicion. "Who are you?" He demanded brusquely.

"The park supervisor." Simon was too astonished by the visitor to protest at his behaviour. "Who are *you*?"

"Police." The other replied tersely, probing the room with his eyes. "Have you been here long?"

"What, worked here you mean?" Simon was still too sleepy to grasp the significance of the intruder's question. "A year or two. Why?"

The other had stridden across to the window, and was looking out across the nursery garden beyond. He turned with a sigh of exasperation. "How long have you been sitting in that chair?"

"Oh." Simon consulted his watch. "About three quarters of an hour I suppose."

"And no one's come in here during that time?"

"Only you. Why?"

"A man was stabbed in your park not half an hour ago. Chummy, who did it, was seen heading this way."

"Oh!" The supervisor was certainly awake now. "What does he look like?"

"Slim build, five foot ten or eleven tall, wearing a blue tracksuit and a khaki hood of some sort, so the two witnesses say."

"That sounds almost like a description of our flasher."

"Doesn't it just." The other agreed grimly.

"But I thought you'd caught him." Simon didn't know Carol's lover by sight and hadn't Len to inform him of Tom's presence in the park.

"So did we squire; but it seems we might have made a cockup of it all. The poor bastard who got stabbed by chummy was our major suspect until now. So we're all going to be left with egg on our faces unless we catch the real one this time; which I won't do by standing here talking to you." He paused with his fingers resting on the handle of the door. "Get in touch with us if you do see anything suspicious won't you?"

"Of course." Simon promised the departing back as he consulted his watch once again. Twenty past one. There was still ten minutes of his dinner hour to go. He snuggled back into his chair, closed his eyes....and opened then again suddenly as a muffled sneeze sounded somewhere in his office.

"Who's there?" The supervisor demanded nervously, but there was no reply. "Who is it?"

A second sneeze filled the room, then a third and a fourth, followed by the emergence from behind a cupboard set across an angle of the wall, of a dusty figure of slim build, about five feet ten or eleven tall, clad in a tracksuit and hood.

The startled Spaulding leapt to his feet, making a grab for an iron bar leaning against the defunct radiator at the side of his chair.

"Wait!" The second intruder implored him, between further uncontrollable bouts of sneezing. "It isn't what it seems. I can explain everything."

7

Councillor Warren Hescott smiled grimly to himself as he passed the young cedar marked by a plaque stating, incorrectly, that he had planted it in commemoration of his years of service to the borough. He had a meeting arranged for the following day, with the Assistant Director (Parks) and his Maintenance Manager (South), at which he intended to state just what he thought of them.

The councillor did not consider himself to be a vindictive man, but the ignominy of his mode of arrival at the tree planting ceremony still rankled, and though he was fit enough now to take up jogging again he did not intend to forgive or forget. At least one head should roll for what had happened to him, he had decided. Hinting over the phone to Gormann that the head should preferably belong to John Death. Gormann, in reply, had intimated that Simon Spaulding was a more suitable sacrifice from his point of view, and this the old man had agreed to accept. He didn't feel any animosity towards the supervisor, but honour had to be satisfied after all.

Hescott jogged on a little further, intending to trot up the slope to the cascade and then down the path beyond, when a cyclist coming towards him suddenly braked hard and kicked out wildly at something hidden from Hescott by a screen of low growing scrub.

Warren knew only too well what that meant. That infernal dog was up to its tricks again. Considering discretion to be by far the better part of valour, he turned away from his usual route around the lake and went down a narrow path, fringed on either side by hazel and field maple bushes, which led him into the woods in the vicinity of Chestnut Square.

It was not a thing the councillor would ever admit to, and few people would have dared even suggest it to the irascible old devil, but he had been becoming increasingly deaf of late. It was because of this that he heard neither the screams, which had alerted Tom Stone and Arnold Lovett, nor the sirens of the police summoned by an urgent phone call from an anxious Carol. The first Hescott knew of the pandemonium in the park was when a burly uniformed figure broke cover a few yards further along the path, stared at the approaching jogger in apparent disbelief, then came full pelt towards him gesticulating wildly for support.

Hescott never stopped to consider the reason for his action. He knew only that a large body of policemen was suddenly bearing down on him with ominous intent. With a speed and agility, which surprised the man himself, he leaped the low railings bordering the path, and ran hell for leather in a blind panic that carried him away from the pursuing force.

8

Simon weighed up the story carefully when the old man had finished telling it. On the whole he tended to believe what he had heard. Hescott seemed an unlikely candidate to be the flasher though, on the other hand, he *was* unusually fit for his age.

"It wasn't me Simon." The councillor noticed the sudden doubt in the other man's eyes. "I simply panicked and ran. It's something that could happen to anyone." Even to Tom Stone, he thought chastenedly. "That damn dog was to blame."

Spaulding smiled. "Sammy? He's a friendly old thing. Just hates cyclists and joggers, that's all. About the tree planting though." Thought of the dog awoke a grievance. "Are you intending to go ahead with your complaint over what happened?"

"Yes." Opponents would have recognised the stubborn jutting of Hescott's jaw as a warning to be wary about how they continued.

"You know that I'm to take the can back for any complaint you make, don't you?"

"Gormann did mention something of the sort." Hescott admitted airily. "His usual sort of bluster to get himself off the hook it seemed to me."

"I've been told to make myself available when you have your meeting with him tomorrow."

"Oh?" The councillor, already fully aware of that, adopted a nonchalant tone, which irritated his companion into a disconcerting revelation.

"It occurred to me that I might spend the time whilst I'm waiting writing out a report of what happened here today. Somebody is bound to ask me and I don't want to forget any of the details when they do. By the way - does your name have one T or two?"

Warren considered his options carefully. In all his years he'd never given in to blackmail, either in politics or in business, but he had to concede that Simon had him over a barrel this time. The councillor had to smile at that. How could he help but admire the way in which Spaulding had summed up the situation and smoothly manipulated it to his own advantage? It reminded Warren of himself in the early days.

Of course, his thoughts raced on, no one would believe that he was the Middleton Hall rapist and any charge, if brought, could be easily disproved. On the other hand, dirt stuck once it had been thrown and, deserve it or not, people would always associate him with the charge in the future and cast their votes accordingly.

He conceded defeat with a sigh. "Perhaps I was a little hasty in my judgement Simon. If you're kind you'll put it down to the loss of dignity clouding my mind. Old sods like me haven't much else going for them besides that and if you rob them of it well..." He held out his hand to the younger man. "I don't really want to damage your career."

"That's just how I feel about yours' councillor." Simon accepted the gesture with relief.

9

John Death was not so happy with the turn of events when he heard about them from Peter Gormann, early the next morning. "Called off the meeting?" He scraped some of the dottle from the bowl of his pipe with a cocktail stick he kept for the purpose. Depositing it in the waste tin at his feet. "Postponed it you mean?"

"Cancelled it altogether." Gormann corrected his maintenance manager's supposition. "Had a change of heart apparently and decided to let the whole thing drop."

"Damn!" Death snapped the cocktail stick in his agitation. "There's no chance of him changing his mind I suppose?"

"No. We're off the hook this time." The assistant director completely missed the point of Death's question. "You'd better let Spaulding know the councillor's decision. He'll be relieved to know he's in the clear I should imagine. Now, about this business of the gross over-expenditure in your nurseries....." Death shelved all thoughts of a further attack on Simon whilst he mustered up an impregnable defence for himself.

CHAPTER TWENTY

The following days were trying ones for Carol, as an unconscious Tom Stone faltered on the brink of death. The borough had a sliding scale of eligibility for compassionate leave depending on the closeness of the blood relationship between petitioner and patient. Lovers did not appear anywhere on the scale and Tom's condition should not have entitled Carol to any concessions at all. The blind eye Simon turned to several absences from the nursery taken by the distrait woman did allow her to maintain a lonely vigil at the hospital. It was lucky for all concerned that John Death was still tied up by problems of his own, though, and unaware of the use Simon was making of the resultant relaxed vigilance.

The appearance at the hospital of someone the nurses addressed as Mrs Stone came as a considerable shock to Carol. Apart from the single occasion when Tom had let slip the fact of her existence, there had never been any mention of her, and Carol had come to treat her as a comfortably mythological figure. To find herself superseded in importance, so far as the medical staff at the hospital were concerned, by this creature whose closeness to her Tom she was unsure of, was a little too much for Carol to accept without question. The more so when it became clear that the woman was the recipient of much sympathetic attention from doctors and nurses, whilst she herself seemed to be there on sufferance alone.

The two women haunted the hospital waiting room and corridors for days, but though each knew well enough who the other was, and the role which she served in the sick man's life, not a word ever passed between them. Whether spending hours over cups of the dark liquid which passed there as tea, slipping out of the building for a nervous cigarette, as Mrs Stone frequently did, or simply sitting turning things over in their minds, each acted as if the other woman didn't exist.

When a little Sri Lankan nurse brought the news that Tom had regained consciousness and wished to see her, Carol experienced a ridiculous sense of triumph over her rival. Mrs Stone rode the snub well, however. Her only reaction being to shrug and turn her back to stare out of the window at a depressing scene of rambling roofs and abandoned courtyards.

Sunk into pillows made grey by the pallor of his face, Stone smiled painfully up at the trembling Carol as she entered the small private room off the main ward where he lay. "We got 'im girl," he whispered with such satisfaction that Carol hadn't the heart to break the news that the hooded man had escaped again. "Now they'll 'ave to believe in me innocence."

The nurse ran an expert eye over the paraphernalia of bottles and tubing attached to her patient. "Ten minutes only." She warned Carol as she left.

What do I say to him? The desperate thought filled Carol's mind as she found herself alone at last with her man. Situations such as this invariably filled her with panic. Fleeing from the silence between them she ran, as ever, into the foolish. "Does it hurt very much?" She cringed inwardly at the absurdity of the question.

Stone shrugged as best he could. "Not too much." The pain etched in his face belied the words. "Werf it anyway." He added. "Proved me innocence din' I? An' got the bleeder into the bargain. Can't complain about a little bit of pain after that."

Again Carol shied from the opportunity of telling him the truth. Instead she asked, "Did you know your wife is here?"

"Sharon? Yeh. They told me, but I didn't wanna see 'er. Why should I? She ain't bin near me for months now. Well you know. Told yer about 'er didn' I?"

"No Tom you didn't," Carol answered quietly, "but it doesn't matter now." She noticed the spasm of pain run through his body. "Do you want the nurse?" Her finger hovered over the bedside button.

"No." Tom relaxed again with a sigh. He was feeling light-headed and detached from the world. Floating almost. He knew he must bring himself back to earth long enough to explain. "Nufin' to trouble 'er for. Besides, she'd 'ave yer leavin', an' I gotta tell yer about Sharon," his eyes clouded with uncertainty. "I 'aven' told yer about 'er already 'ave I? Only I can't seem to remember."

"No Tom, you haven't, but it really isn't important now. It'll keep until you're better."

"Maybe," he answered in a way that made her blood run cold, "but I'd rarver get it off me chest now. It concerns us - you an' me that is - a lot.

You see, everyfin' that 'appened between us, 'appened because of Sharon. She left me - for the milkman as it 'appens - because she reckoned I wasn't no good in bed. I fought it was a joke when she told me. I mean! There 'andn't been an inklin' that there was anyfin' wrong in that way. I fought - well I fought I done all right in that line until then. Afterwards, though, I wondered, an' when I done wonderin', - cause it ain't the kind of fin' you wanna discuss wiv yer mates - I started readin' - well you know the sort of books I mean - to see if there *was* somefin' in what she'd said. After fifteen years of marriage she 'ad me doin' that!

It was durin' the finkin' stage that I first noticed you around the park. Fancied yer like, but, after what Sharon'd done to me, I didn't 'ave the nerve to take a chance.

The readin' got me finkin' though. I'd always been a man for straight sex but well... you know what I done? I wrote to one of them problem pages an' asked about it. Muriel Bainbridge. I felt a right fool at the time, but it worked out, what she said."

"Nothing that takes place between two consenting adults in private is wrong," Carol caught herself quoting quietly. "I'm sorry," she told the surprised Tom, "it's a long story. Finish yours first, then I'll tell you."

"Not much more to say. I found the courage from somewhere to chat yer. An' took it from there. I was worried though. I mean, you didn't bat an eye at anyfin' I suggested. Too sophisticated for you, she is, I kept tellin' meself. She'll pack yer like Sharon done if yer let on that this ain't really yer style. So I kept finkin' of new fings to do an' 'opin' you'd never catch on that I wasn't for real."

"Oh Tom." Carol breathed. "If you'd only known."

"I was never an artist neiver. That was another lie. I couldn't paint to save me life, but I didn't wanna admit to yer that I was on the dole, an' I fought bein' an artist would account for me wanderin' about all frough the day. I fought it might impress yer a bit as well. Silly really. Should 'ave told yer I was a photographer. I always could take a good picture. 'Ad one published once. Didn't know that, did yer girl? In a magazine it was. A picture of you. I was really proud of that, but I never got the chance to tell yer 'cause yer started to freeze me out about then, an' I figured yer must 'ave sussed me, an' were givin' me the big E."

"Oh no Tom." Sudden realisation tortured the listening woman.

"You'd better leave now." The nurse spoke at Carol's shoulder.

"But I want to explain," she protested pleadingly. "Can't I have a few more minutes?"

"They'd be wasted if you did." The nurse took her gently by the arm and Carol, turning for a last look at her lover, saw Tom had slipped away into sleep.

"He will get better, won't he?" Carol asked, as she allowed herself to be led from the room. "He isn't going to die?"

"I'm afraid you must ask sister that." Came the disconcerting reply and for the second time during that visit Carol experienced a cold fear.

2

Gerald Wilson was also afraid but, unlike Carol, his fears were of his own making. He had finally returned to work after a prolonged absence, but his hopes that he had overcome his problem had been dashed the instant he set foot between the automatic doors of the Civic Centre. A million traumas and hang-ups had rushed to greet him like a long lost friend.

Somehow he had made it to his desk, where he now sat drawing in deep breaths, as his doctor had advised him, but still the walls of the office advanced and receded around him and the conversations of better adjusted colleagues beat relentlessly against his ears. The maintenance co-ordinator felt the perspiration break out all over his body in a display of terror he was unable to contain.

"Gerald! Gerald!" Peter Gormann leaned across Wilson's desk and spoke urgently to the older man.

The latter broke free of the spell that bound him. "I-I'm s-sorry Peter. I was... was...." he was surprised to find that the effort of speaking had left him short of breath.

"Snap out of it man!" Gormann urged him. "What's the matter with you?"

"I-I r-really d-don't f-feel v-very well. P-perh-haps I c-came b-back to w-work t-t-too s-soon."

"Not bloody soon enough, I'd say." Gormann contradicted him unsympathetically. "You get stuck into these malingering ways of yours and your effectiveness as a part of the management team will become a thing of the past so far as I'm concerned.

I've a meeting with Potter in ten minutes to thrash out Death's projected spending on the Middleton nursery. I want your support in cutting it by at least a third."

"I-I d-don't t-think I-I c-can o-o-of-f-fer a-any."

"Bosh man! Pull yourself together! Do you want Death stepping into your shoes?"

"What do you mean?" The unexpected suggestion shocked Wilson out of his stutter.

"Isn't it obvious? You've become the weak link in the management chain Gerald. The office joke. Damn it all! None of this over expenditure on nurseries could have happened if you'd been here to monitor it."

"I was sick." Wilson interposed with wounded dignity.

"You weren't here," Gormann replied brutally, "for whatever reason, and John Death manoeuvred the okay from Potter to take on some of your duties in your absence. That's how he sneaked the money from other codes without anyone catching on until now and you have to take responsibility for that.

I'm sympathetic towards you Gerald. I've covered up a lot of your ineptitude in the past, hoping you'd pull out of this decline, but enough is enough. You're paid to do a job and from now on I expect you to do it.

The meeting starts in," he consulted his watch, "seven minutes. I want you there and I expect all the support I require of you to carry the day. Otherwise we'll have to start thinking in terms of a less responsible position for you, and I wonder what Eileen would say to that?"

Left alone, Wilson subsided into panic. It was all very well for Peter to tell him to pull himself together, but that wasn't such an easy thing to do. How could he help it if his mind always froze when faced by a problem with which he was unable to cope? How was he supposed to sort out technical difficulties of crafts in which he had had no basic training? Modern thinking might suggest that a manager managed and had no need of any knowledge of the basics of what he managed. Modern thinking hadn't taken into account that facing the likes of John Death without the comfort of equal knowledge was like facing a tank with only a knife for protection. Fine for Gormann to talk! He had a training in horticulture to fall back on. All right for Eileen to keep pushing! She only had to spend the money, not earn it."

"Excuse me Gerald."

"Yes?" Wilson looked up from his dilemma to meet the eyes of a small blonde girl who stood smiling down at him. Linda Gainsborough was the newest and prettiest of the technical assistants. Before his recent bout of sickness Gerald had often taken his tea break with her. There was something sympathetic and relaxing about Linda. Perhaps it was her attitude towards him. There weren't many people left in the co-ordinator's life who didn't treat him with amusement or contempt.

"I don't know if you can help me. I'm having trouble with my car. You see it won't start properly and the engine makes a terrible noise when it does. At home I'd get my brother to look at it," Linda had moved to London from Derbyshire, having qualified at a local horticultural college, "but he can't come down here at the moment and I can't afford to put it into a garage with charges the way they are. I'd try to do something about it myself, of course, but I'm completely lost when it comes to anything to do with machinery. Ray Bradman," Wilson shot a look at the senior technical assistant, who grinned back at him with malicious pleasure, "tells me you're an expert though. He said you'd be bound to want to have a look at it just to keep your hand in. What do you think? I'd be most awfully grateful for any help you could offer."

On the brink of a curt refusal to become the butt of Bradman's spiteful sense of humour, the maintenance co-ordinator felt an unexpected spark of resistance flare up inside him. The office joke. Gormann had called him that and now the supercilious Bradman was pressing home the point. And what was he? What was Gormann? Or even Death if you looked at him dispassionately? Posers. Con men. My trouble is that I'm too open, Wilson thought to himself, too honest for my own good; but that could change.

His mind made up, he smiled back at the hopeful Linda. There was no dismissing her attractions lightly and Eileen *had* been feeling her age these past few months.

"I'd be happy to look at it for you," he replied equably, "though I can't promise that I'll be able to do more than offer advice.

Supposing we go for a drive this lunchtime and I'll see if I can pinpoint the trouble from the sound of the engine. We'll be in a better position then to see what can be done."

"Fine." The girl swayed engagingly back across the office towards her drawing board and the thwarted Bradman.

Gerald gave the latter an expansive smile, then gathered up all the papers on his desk he thought might be appropriate to the meeting with Potter. Be damned to it, he thought to himself, it was time that there was the possibility of some pleasure in his life. Too much work and no play at all was certainly making Jack a candidate for a breakdown. It was time to see what a reversal of his priorities could do for him.

The prospect was so stimulating that a renewed Wilson took the meeting by storm, allowing a bemused John Death to escape with only half his proposed budget still intact. It said much for Wilson's performance that Death considered himself lucky to have got away with that.

3

The loss of their projected spending power had little effect on the Middleton Hall staff, since none of them had been aware of the chance of it being available to them in the first place. Interest there continued to centre on more mundane aspects of daily life. The humour of Len Saunders being a typical case in point.

Len had returned from his leave an angry man. There were those, such as Lovett, who might have argued that this was his usual state, but they were biased men. Len was capable of a black humour on favourable occasions; but this was not one of those. He stumped into the mess room and signed his name on the attendance sheet without a word, stopping only to silence Henry's jovial enquiry about his holiday with a look.

Out of sight of Len, a knowing look passed between the other men present. Obviously the senior attendant had not enjoyed his time away. It remained for Simon Spaulding to face up to the other's dark mood and find out why.

"You know where I went of course?" Simon, who had a very shrewd idea where, declined to answer and Saunders went on, "Bledstock, to see Melody's family.

You should meet them Simon. The newspapers are always on about a society that doesn't care. Well those two personify it. They bloody do! Hours I've spent with them this past week and I still don't know what makes them tick.

Her old man is so bloody self-righteous that he wouldn't even listen to what I had to say. Seemed to stick at the idea that I was in the same boat as Melody because I was trying to help her and refused to budge from it. And as for the mother! So prim and proper all the time that he was in the room. Bowing and scraping and hanging on his every word. If he'd wanted to pick his nose she'd have offered him her finger to do it with. Once he was out of earshot she let slip that she came down here hoping to see Melody about the time of the last plant sale. Seems she missed the kid, but had a chat to Carol instead, so we know now how Maggot found out about Melody. Bloody Carol opening her mouth for once. God I was glad to get away from that narrow minded little town and its bigoted inhabitants! I could see why Melody couldn't stay there once her secret was out."

"You heard about Carol's bloke I suppose?" Simon made a move to steer his companion away from a topic he had no great desire to pursue.

"What? Oh - yes I did. Rough luck on him, but who'd have thought that our flasher would suddenly turn vicious? It only goes to show that it doesn't pay to try to be a hero."

"It paid Arnold." The attendant had received an extensive write up in the local press and influential people in Middleton were trying to get him an award of some sort for his rescue of Tom Stone.

"That's bloody typical of course." Saunders remarked gloomily. "Lovett of all people. If ever a man deserved bad fortune it's him, and yet that silly sod goes and stabs the other poor bastard instead. How's Carol taking it?"

"Keeping her feelings in check."

"Poor cow." Len mused sympathetically for a moment. "Anything else I ought to know?"

Simon had dreaded the admission, which must follow that question, but it couldn't be put off any longer. He didn't know why he felt so guilty about it anyway. It wasn't as if he was personally responsible.

"Melody's gone." He tried not to catch Len's eye as he spoke. "She's not been seen since the day of the suicide. I've asked around but....It seems she vanished into thin air."

"I should have thought the air was thick in Manchester. It seemed it last time I was there."

"What?" The thought crossed Simon's mind that his news had unhinged Len, but he dismissed it almost immediately as being unlikely.

Saunders took an envelope from his pocket and brandished it at his supervisor as if that, itself, explained everything. "Melody's in Manchester with that lanky WPC who used to patrol through here. Seems they got together somehow and decided they were meant for each other.

I found this letter waiting for me when I got home. That was what really made my trip worthwhile. She says she's finally found someone she can trust. Someone who was happy to give up everything for her without even being asked. Seems to hint that I had the chance to do the same and let it slip. Says they've gone north to make a fresh start away from everyone who knew them before and thanks me for all I did for her when she was here. She asks to be remembered to you as well." He crumpled the envelope thoughtfully. "It all seems a bit strange to me. What do you think?"

"What? Asking to be remembered to me? A bit tactless perhaps, but not so very strange."

"Not that Simon!" Saunders snapped irritably. "I meant them shacking up together. Is that normal?"

Simon shrugged. "How normal was the life she was leading in the first place?"

"Not very, I suppose." The other acknowledged. "But I've been making enquiries about this WPC Mackenzie. The cop in the panda reckons she's bent. He says she was well known at the station as a man hater. So it seems as if Melody, who's a boy wanting to be a girl, has set up home with a girl who doesn't like boys. All of which is long way from normal in my book." He fell into a brown study for a moment, emerging with a rueful smile. "Ah well, I suppose it's for the best that she's gone.

How did you get on with Hescott?" He changed the subject quite deliberately. The way things were shaping when I left, I thought you'd have been packed off before I got back."

"For a while it seemed that way to me too." Simon admitted with a grin. "In the end he decided to drop all charges though, and I was left without a stain on my character."

"I bet Death wasn't too happy about that. Why did Hescott do it?"

Simon tapped the side of his nose. "Can't tell you that I'm afraid Len. Promised the councillor I wouldn't. As for Death. Wilson is chasing him so much lately he hasn't the time to worry what I'm doing."

"Wilson?" Saunders echoed incredulously.

"Our Gerald's discovered a new lease of life lately. Even got himself a bit on the side from somewhere."

"Go on!"

"Henry saw them up along the river bank when he went to watch courting couples the other dinnertime. Large as life and twice as active so he says."

"Does his missus know do you reckon?"

"I shouldn't think so. He's looking too pleased with himself at the moment for that. Wait till she does find out though!"

"That'll give him a real reason for nervous debility." The smile on the senior attendant's face died as he recognised an approaching figure. "And here comes another reason for it."

"You're back then Mr Saunders?" Arnold Lovett strolled up to the two men, his broom over his shoulder.

"I am Arnold." Len agreed heavily. "Just in time to say goodbye to you, I shouldn't wonder."

"You're leaving us then?" The other asked in genuine surprise.

"Don't be bloody silly!" Saunders exploded. "I meant that you were."

"I'm not going anywhere. Am I Mr Spaulding?" He appealed to the supervisor.

"I think Len was under the impression you'd have no reason to stay now the cockerel's been found." The latter explained. "I hadn't got around to telling him about your new interest."

"Not actually new." Lovett corrected him. "Just a variation on the old one really. It's metal detecting," he explained to the silent Saunders. "Something I got into as a side line to trying to find that dratted cockerel.

I've had a chat to the ministry people, and they've given me permission to run my detector over their yards as long as I chart the positive responses and get the okay from them before I actually dig for anything.

I'm hoping the borough council will agree a similar arrangement with me. I've already written to Mr Potter for permission. I don't think he'll refuse once he understands the Ministry have said yes.

Just think of all the things that must be buried in these grounds. Coins, weapons, jewellery," his eyes gleamed at the prospect. "I can hardly wait to begin."

"Simon!" Saunders turned imploringly to Spaulding, who simply shrugged. "You can't let it happen! There'll be holes everywhere. At least we always knew where to look for him before. Now he'll be turning up all over the place.

Look here," he stabbed a bony forefinger in the junior man's chest, "I don't give a toss what Potter or the Ministry tell you. If I catch you digging up the park I'll..."

"There isn't a thing you'll be able to do about it once I get permission."

From a distance, Maggot watched the escalation of the argument with appreciative interest. Still harbouring a grudge against Simon and Len for the part he suspected them of playing in his recent incapacity, he welcomed anything with the potential to make trouble for them in their turn.

Maggot's aspirations to become supervisor might be in the doldrums after his failure to measure up to the demands John Death had made of him, but he still had no doubt in his own mind that the call *would* come.

4

In the hospital Carol still sat patiently awaiting some sign of improvement in the condition of her stricken Tom. The rasping of his laboured breathing as he struggled to survive becoming the entire world she knew.

It was all the more surprising then that a full minute had elapsed before the overwhelming silence of the room awoke the weeping woman to her loss.

The End

If you have enjoyed this book why not read Brian W Taylor's other books available on line as e-books from Amazon Kindle and paperback books from Amazon.

Why Weeps the Willow - a restless spirit seeks to find a way of experiencing again the physical love she enjoyed with her lover when she was still alive.

Let Sleeping Evils Lie – a midnight vigil in a churchyard by students trying to contact a ghost said to haunt it, and some impromptu dabbling with an Ouija board in a youth club a few days later, awaken a sleeping evil it would have been better to leave undisturbed.

Murder in the Marches– a girl looking for her father, who disappeared piloting his own plane across Wales, finds out more about him than she bargained for in a love story with a background of drug smuggling across the Welsh Marches.

The Body in the Woods - The body of a man slumped beside the ruins of a house in the woods, whispering dying words about a 'Destroying Angel'.
The body of another man laying in the cottage the first man had lived in; clutching a package to his chest he'd stolen from someone who had just killed him in an unsuccessful attempt to get it back.
No good retiring to Shropshire if it's a *quiet* life you're looking for. Not as long as Chief Inspector Macdonald is still there pulling the strings.

Murder Through Mischance - A man pushed to his death from a cliff in Mallorca. After taking photographs of someone he saw at a village fiesta there. The body of a second man found in the outhouse of a cottage in Shropshire, whose death seems to be linked in some way to that of the first. Is it true that there might be a third body? That Chief Inspector Macdonald has finally been taken out of the game? Or is he still there where he always was? In the background, pulling the strings.

Haunted Hearts - Nobody really believed the grounds of Moorecroft House in Shropshire were haunted. That was just a story someone had made up once to draw the punters in wasn't it? Who then was the man in Elizabethan costume who appeared so suddenly out of the mist early one morning? What was he doing there? And how much truth was there in the story he had to tell? A story of a love affair which ended with a violent murder. A murder for which the wrong person paid the ultimate price.

Printed in Great Britain
by Amazon